Charles Leonard Moore

**Banquet of Palacios**

A Comedy

Charles Leonard Moore

**Banquet of Palacios**
*A Comedy*

ISBN/EAN: 9783744784207

Printed in Europe, USA, Canada, Australia, Japan

Cover: Foto ©Andreas Hilbeck / pixelio.de

More available books at **www.hansebooks.com**

Charles Leonard Moore

**Banquet of Palacios**
*A Comedy*

ISBN/EAN: 9783744784207

Printed in Europe, USA, Canada, Australia, Japan

Cover: Foto ©Andreas Hilbeck / pixelio.de

More available books at **www.hansebooks.com**

# BANQUET OF PALACIOS.

## A COMEDY.

BY

CHARLES LEONARD MOORE.

C. L. MOORE,
305 WALNUT STREET, PHILADELPHIA.
1889.

# PERSONS.

PEDRO PALACIOS.
JUAN FLORES FALCON.
PADRE PACIFICO.
PADRE CYPRIAN.
LIEUTENANT ESPIRITU SANTOS DE LA TORRE.
SEÑOR HERRARA.
SEÑOR BARBOZA.
MARQUIS LUNA DE SILVA.
JOSE CAVALHO.
LUIS ALVES.
APPARITIO.
TITAN PAPE.
SEÑORA FEREIRA HERRARA.
JASMIN.
ERÈRÈ.
CERITA.

*Boy, Officers, Servants, etc.*

Place of drama, Para, at the mouth of the Amazons. Time, the present.

# Banquet of Palacios.

## Scene I.

*A hut in Para.* Cerita *in a hammock.*

*Falcon.* (*Without.*)  Cerita!

*Cerita.* (*Waking.*)  A  spider's
web woven o'er my face!  What
noise is that?  Who calls?

*Falcon.*  Flores,  Cerita;  your
brother Flores!

*Cerita.* And I dreaming of dis-
asters.  Oh, Flores, my door should
dance itself open to you.

*Falcon.* Hold, my child!  Not so
fast.  The door is well enough as it
is.  My planet is in occultation.
My dwelling-place is the extreme
dark.

*Cerita.* What do you mean, Flores? What mischief make-believe are you at?

*Falcon.* Alas, I pretend nothing. I am absolutely simple. Cerita, you know Señor Cavalho, my host, the landlord of the Hotel Belem?

*Cerita.* What, that round, red, flaming gentleman! Know him; why, I wash for him. Nobody in Para has such clean linen as he. I do it out of gratitude because of his kindness to you.

*Falcon.* Gratitude, Cerita; I am damned with gratitude. I have been at his charges now for eighteen months and only hopes have paid the score. My bill has fattened faster than I. It is swollen by the dropsy of interest,—twelve per cent. a month and a percentage upon that per cent. By Our Lady, Cerita, I am a sum in compound interest. Simple as I stand here I have eaten off him until I am the sole asset of his establishment. I represent a herd of oxen, forty sheep, and a whole poultry-yard of hens and pigeons. Why, I can crow and flap my wings—so. At the last day I shall resolve back into these my elements. The Lord shall see herds coming out of me, every separate winged or walking thing of them, stamped with the inscription "Jose Cavalho."

*Cerita.* But, Flores, if it is as bad as this, why don't he send you away?

*Falcon.* I am grown too valuable. I am the whole savings of the poor man's lifetime. Why, he turns pale if I sit in a draught, and if I take a third glass of wine he sends for the doctor. 'Tis a new fear to have one's bank threatened with apoplexy. He borrows money on me, and I go about like a bill of exchange. I am attended by a retinue in the daytime, and at night my groom of the chamber carries off my clothes for the better security of my person. And that is why I keep the door closed.

*Cerita.* Why, Flores, you are not——

*Falcon.* Bare as a statue, naked as a handful of water. Night is my only tailor. I have bolted from my prison of hospitality. I am free though unfeathered. My soul leaps within me. Oh, Cerita, let me recite you a poem.

*Cerita.* But, Flores, you are cold. I hear you shivering. And then, some one may see you.

*Falcon.* Cerita, the night-dews are glittering on me, but the sun is just about to shake its eastern gates apart. In five minutes I shall be observed. I ask you for friendship and a pair of trousers.

*Cerita.* Why, yes! Here is a

linen suit belonging to Lieutenant Espiritu Santos de la Torre. He will not expect it for a week. Open and take it.

*Falcon.* What do they do in heaven for angels, Cerita? God be praised that Lieutenant Santos in his conceit of greatness makes his tailor measure him for his rank rather than for his person. His garments are as wide as the great Plaza.

*Cerita.* I had better be godmother to a brood of parrots, or even Our Lady of the Chapel with forty thousand diseases to cure, than sister to such a mischief-making innocent as this. Wit crept into his brain once and pushed wisdom out of doors, and so I've had to dance.

*Enter* FALCON.

*Falcon.* Behold me, Cerita, bristling with brilliancy. (*Pompously.*) Do not take me for an immortal, child, for well I know that 'tis I who look upon immortal things,—youth and beauty and unfailing love.

*Cerita.* La, sir, how you talk to a poor washerwoman. But are you really my brother Flores? Why, the boy is beautiful.

*Falcon.* The sun is in the air and hope is in my heart. Oh, I can hear my blood sing! I am free! I am young! Dance, Cerita, dance! Oh, I must recite you a poem! Where is my breakfast?

*Cerita.* There isn't any.

*Falcon.* None. What did you do with that fish I sent you a week ago?

*Cerita.* I lived off of it two days. Then, if the neighbors had not taken it away, I should have had to move.

*Falcon.* Fool, ass that I am, why do I talk of breakfasts? I will get you breakfast, dinner, a year of banquets. My troubles have driven prosperity from my head. Do you know that yesterday I finished my great book, Silves Amazonas? Before the ink was dry I had it at Señor Barboza's, the publisher. You know him? He is very wise, for he has been saving up his wit for half a century with his mouth shut. He broods on great thoughts and begets them. He sits on his authors as a hen does on eggs and each one hatches out a phœnix. I did not see him, but I left my book, and I think he sat up all night to read it. As soon as it is decently daylight he will send me a letter of praise and a purse of money.

*Cerita.* Dear, generous man.

*Falcon.* Generous! Well, he has a bargain. That is all right, and now I have another confidence for you. I met a girl in the market-place yesterday. What are you laughing at? There's nothing odd in a girl. It was this way. Titan Pape, the old Cearense beggar, was being jostled by the crowd. I sprang forward to help him, when up rose at his right hand a vision, girl or angel, I know not which, and drew him away. She had on a sheepskin robe, and that in rags, so that you could see she was made of solid ivory. Her eyes——

*Cerita.* Yes, I know. Her eyes, crystalline fountains, glassing golden stars. Her lips, rose-petals by their perfume pushed apart. Her hair——

*Falcon.* Why, where did you get those epithets, sister?

*Cerita.* Out of those verses you made me carry Señorita Jasmin yesterday. Oh, Flores, let me recite you a poem.

*Falcon.* Jasmin! Faith, Cerita, all my astronomy is for twin stars. Erèrè, Jasmin, Jasmin, Erèrè, which shall it be? Shall I toss for a choice? Have you a coin, Cerita, to play Œdipus to this riddle?

*Cerita.* 'Tis my last one, Flores. But some one knocks. Enter, Señor.

### *Enter* Boy.

Oh, Flores, here is your fortune.

*Boy.* Señor Barboza returns you this package, Señor.

*Falcon.* My manuscript, and unopened! But the letter, the letter!

*Boy.* I have no letter, nothing but the package.

*Falcon.* Oh, very well. Here's to pay your trouble.

*Boy.* Thank you, Señor.    [*Exit.*

*Cerita.* Flores, why do you stare so stupidly? Say something, or I will shake you.

*Falcon.* Is this all? My book, my Silves Amazonas, is this your treatment? Ye sunny water-glades, ye cool wood interiors, ye gaudy-colored haciendas, ye seringeiro huts set on a single post like a stork on one leg, ye fisher-folk, ye brown girls with only one garment which somebody else is wearing half the time, ye fat Padres deep in the dialectics of drink, ye festas and religious processions, all the pictured visions of my life, is this your treatment? Now the world shall pay for this. I write no more.

*Cerita.* Oh, Flores, do not grieve. This is but a moment's misfortune. Envy strikes in the dark at you.

*Falcon.* Do you think so, Cerita? I always valued your opinion. This may be malice.

*Cerita.* Not a doubt of it.

*Falcon.* Then I'm damned if I don't write. There's matter in my head. I will begin, straightway, to-night, a poem of one hundred thousand lines. The world shall suffer for this.

*Cerita.* Ay, my dear brother. That's revenge.

*Falcon.* Cerita, you shall judge. Listen to this piece; 'tis a pastoral of Monte Alegre.

*Cerita.* By Our Lady, no! Flores, I do not mind having nothing to eat, but poetry makes me thin. Besides, I have got to go out and get some breakfast for you.

*Falcon.* Breakfast! Beautiful! But how, Cerita? I gave your last coin away.

*Cerita.* Why, you know this is Beggars' Saturday. Any one is privileged to beg to-day. I have a disguise here in the corner. See, I put on this sheepskin cloak and leather hat and forthwith I am a Cearense exile, and sure to pouch a pound of coppers before you can make three good wishes. Farewell, fair brother.

[*Exit.*

*Falcon.* Adios, dear child. Flores,

if it were night, you and I would go
out and sit on the rocks in the river
and think till we slipped off. Being
day, we had best make a good reso-
lution and hang ourself. What the
devil! my body belongs to Señor
Cavalho and my clothes to Lieutenant Santos. There's nothing of my
own but my soul. Hanging cannot
hurt the soul. Yet hold! Laying
violent hands on another man's
property is theft. Well, then, I do
not take their effects away: only
withdraw what is my own. Clearly,
hanging was invented for my case.
Come, can I find a rope. Ay, this
hammock-cord will do.

*Enter* JOSE CAVALHO, *bursting through the
door.*

*Cavalho.* Is Señor Falcon—— Oh,
my heart! Let me get my breath! I
have run a mile. Is Juan Flores——
I burn, I choke! Air, a fan, a

fan! Will you let me die at your feet? Be sure they fire nine volleys over my grave, for I was a soldier. Oh, a chair! I have not run thus since the battle of Villa Rica! Is Juan Flores Falcon at home? Are you his brother, Señor? A fan, a fan!

*Falcon.* What do you want with a desperate man, Señor Cavalho? Had you been a minute later you had talked with my ghost.

*Cavalho.* What, Flores! You, my mad maker of rhymes! Coo, coo, coo, my dove. Come, my pretty one, and let me embrace you. Infamous rogue, how you have treated me! My voice is hoarse calling you pet names through the streets of Para. What did you run away for? Come back and I will chain you in your room and feed you on turtle and dulces. Remember the twelve hundred milreis you owe me. My apoplexy shall go in your bill.   Beast of a dog, how will you requite my care? When Gil Tirso, the cook, came with his garlic-flavored breath and his large fat tears, and told me you were flown, my heart sank drowning within me and the water bubbled to my eyes.   Oh, how can you repay me my love?

*Falcon.* Behold this rope, Señor. I will pay all my debts with it, down to the debt of nature.

*Cavalho.* What a horribly significant hammock-cord!   No! no! no! Falcon!   Hanging is the worst indiscretion a man can commit.   Come, you only owe me a thousand milreis. You would not hang yourself for a thousand milreis?

*Falcon.* It is inevitable.   My house is at your disposition, Señor, but pray give me five minutes alone.

*Cavalho.* ·Why, man, you know me. 'Twas but a jest about the thousand milreis. Seven hundred is all there is between us. You make my blood run cold with that string.

*Falcon.* Señor, I was half in heaven when you came, and I must be rude to tell you that you delay my bliss.

*Cavalho.* Well, if it must be so, I take my leave. And this commission I have in my pocket must be filled up anew. I wonder who will get the place, Moraes or Silva?

*Falcon.* What commission are you talking about?

*Cavalho.* A commission as third assistant deputy customs officer made out in your name. But you are past caring for such things now. Well, fare you well. Remember me to my debtors in the lower world.

*Falcon.* Not so fast, old boy. If there is any premium paid for me to live, I can dispense with dying as well as any man. Is it true? Have you a place for me?

*Cavalho.* Behold.

*Falcon.* You have seen a wreath of cigarette-smoke? Puff! it rises and dissolves and disappears. That was me. That was the Falcon of the past,—Falcon the poet. He is gone, and the real Falcon, the Falcon of the present, stands before you. The assistant collector of customs, that is; the politician, the friend of the people, the supporter of the government, the deputy, the President of a Province, that is to be. Oh, I will be great. I will lead a revolution. My ships shall sweep past Tabatinga and conquer Peru, and possess the Amazon from its source to the sea. Senor, you know the great island of Marajo? Well, I am thinking of the time when that island shall serve as the pedestal for a vast equestrian statue which shall dominate these rivers and show a hundred miles at sea: a statue which shall bear upon its base the inscription—JUAN FLORES FALCON, DELIVERER OF THE AMAZONS.

*Cavalho.* Deliverer from what, Flores?

*Falcon.* From what? Oh, anything. That doesn't matter.

*Cavalho.* I have made an arrangement, Flores, to draw one-half your salary every month until my account is settled.

*Falcon.* Well thought of, Señor. But I can better the plan. You will become familiar with the paymaster, and 'tis a pity I should interfere. Draw all my salary and advance me two hundred milreis immediately.

*Cavalho.* Do you desire it?

*Falcon.* It is a necessity.

*Cavalho.* Well, you compel me to follies. I will return to my house and send the money to you at once.

*Falcon.* This is business, Señor, yet I am obliged to you.

*Cavalho.* Well, adios. If this day does not do for me, you may be saved. My heart is in my mouth yet, and I am melting away like a spendthrift's fortune. I must go, I must go!                [*Exit.*

*Falcon.* Well, I am snatched from the fire with scarce a smell of brimstone on me. Falcon, I begin to respect you. Evidently I am preserved for great purposes. (*A knock at the door.*) What a timid knock is that! 'Tis a begging knock. Beggars come to a beggar's door. Enter, Señor. How are you, father?

*Enter* TITAN PAPE *and* ERÈRÈ.

What, Titan Pape! Erèrè!

*Erèrè.* Señor, we ask alms.

*Falcon.* Welcome, Señorita! Welcome, Señor! Pray sit you in this hammock, Erèrè. Señor, you take me at an unfortunate time. My house is yet unfurnished. But the designs are all made for a general upholstering. In this corner should be a large wicker-sofa. Here are to be leather chairs. There an arm-chair of silk. I cannot offer you these, Señor, but be seated, I beg you,—sit at large, sit where you will.

*Titan Pape.* Señor, I thank you. Will you not sit first?

*Falcon.* After you. Or if you desire to stand, I am at your service. Well, let us stand.

*Titan Pape.* Oh, Señor, I prefer it.

*Falcon.* My cigarettes are yours, Señor, but I have not got them from the customs wharf—they come from Manaos. Yours, I doubt not, are excellent.

*Titan Pape.* They are, but, alas, this unfortunate child forgot to bring them forth this morning. The heed-less gayety of youth, Señor!

*Falcon.* It is nothing. Señor, do you find this climate agree with you?

*Titan Pape.* Everything that belongs to you is excellent, Señor.

*Falcon.* But do you not long for your home in Ceara?

*Titan Pape.* Home is any place where the government feeds you. I never knew it to rain rice in Ceara.

*Falcon.* But when the government withdraws its support—the milreis a day which it doles out to you exiles—will you not suffer in this strange country? Perhaps you may have to work.

*Titan Pape.* Impossibilities are impossible, Señor.

*Falcon.* But you have a large family to provide for on the government pittance?

*Titan Pape.* Alas, yes! Seven children.

*Falcon.* And this great girl is your eldest daughter? Erèrè is her name, I think?

*Titan Pape.* Erèrè.

*Falcon.* A charming girl. But she eats, Señor. Her teeth are all sound.

*Titan Pape.* A mere trifle.

*Falcon.* Ah, there the father speaks,—one willing to make any sacrifice for those he loves. But we who look on can pity you. Her clothes, the little ornaments she requires, the accomplishments she must possess, how can you provide them all?

*Titan Pape.* I deny her nothing, Senor.

*Falcon.* That may easily be seen. But do you owe no duty to yourself?

*Titan Pape.* Erèrè is a good girl.

*Falcon.* There is nothing in the world better than girls.

*Titan Pape.* She—she rolls my cigarettes for me.

*Falcon.* But you have another daughter?

*Titan Pape.* Erèrè is very beautiful.

*Falcon.* Do you think so?

*Titan Pape.* Her hair is thick.

*Falcon.* Very coarse and uneven.

*Titan Pape.* She is as straight and slender as an assai palm.

*Falcon.* Alas! much too thin.

*Titan Pape.* Her skin is as smooth as the water twenty feet under the surface.

*Falcon.* I don't like that yellowish color.

*Titan Pape.* Why, Señor, I am that color myself!

*Falcon.* Señor, there are doubtless many little things which the government forgets to provide you?

*Titan Pape.* Alas, yes!

*Falcon.* Some clothes, I suppose?

*Titan Pape.* Clothes! No; as you see, I have clothes.

*Falcon.* What is it you lack, then?

*Titan Pape.* Tobacco!

*Falcon.* Nothing more?

*Titan Pape.* A great deal of tobacco.

*Falcon.* How much, Señor?

*Titan Pape.* An arroba of tobacco.

*Falcon.* Oh, Señor, that is extravagant. Consider, **Erèrè** is only fifteen. An arroba of tobacco! Impossible!

*Titan Pape.* An arroba of tobacco.

*Falcon.* Come, two or three rolls.

*Titan Pape.* An arroba of tobacco.

*Falcon.* Why, Señor, that is worth forty milreis. There are a thousand girls in Para—— Are you mad, or do you only make believe? Come, you infect me with your disease. Half your demand and the business is done. The whole or nothing! Well, 'tis a bargain. I was never one to check and chaffer at a price. Do you know Señor Cavalho? I will write you an order on him. Give him this and he will buy you your estate of smoke. [*Exit* TITAN PAPE.] What, you phantom, you last issue of old Pharaoh's dream, have you such alacrity left in you? Your legs clatter like castanets. You disc set edgewise, you swift shadow, hurry or you are late. Faster, faster! there is only one arroba of tobacco left in Para and that is being bargained for. Well, you are out of sight. Now for my purchase. Wonderful Erèrè.

*Erèrè.* My master.

*Enter* LUIS ALVES.

*Alves.* Flores! a thousand pardons! I am not used to knock.

*Falcon.* 'Tis no matter, Luis. This child is my Secretary.

*Alves.* An honorable post, Señorita. Can you read and write?

*Erèrè.* No, Señor.

*Falcon.* 'Tis not necessary. Fame is a matter of memory. I am to write a poem of one hundred thousand lines and she is to remember it.

*Alves.* Poor child! I cannot remember my own verses, and I don't like anybody else's.

*Falcon.* What have you got, Luis, in that roll?

*Alves.* Oh, Flores, something that will please you, something you must praise. 'Tis the design for the water palace in our new Para.

*Falcon.* Have you abandoned the theatre and the cathedral?

*Alves.* For the moment.  A feeling, I know not what, seized me, and I turned to this.  Examine the design.  'Tis beauty trained to use, simplicity made splendid.  The palace fronts for one mile on the harbor.  Its lines are massive, yet ethereally light.  The elevation is flat, yet there are deep recesses where shadows may lurk at mid-day, and the whole façade is enriched with niches, statues, friezes, in infinite procession.  Great stairs sweep from it here and there to the broad paved platform of the quay.  On the ramparts overlooking the bay stand or crouch, in many attitudes, the carved figures of mighty lions.

*Falcon.* Lions? Horses, Luis!

*Alves.* What do you know about it, Flores? The design calls for lions.

*Falcon.* Why, 'tis plain to the poorest imagination. Here on the parapet the horses, a multitude, stand tense, eager, straining with rivalry, their eyes flashing, their forms leaping forth into the air; while below them, in and out, sweep the massy creatures of the sea, with curling manes and flowing limbs, charging, squadron after squadron, to break against your sea-wall here. It must be horses, Luis!

*Alves.* Am I the architect or you, Flores? You do not know what the harmony of the plan requires. I think I have mastered my art.

*Falcon.* You will master no art until you master your conceit. What! will you compare your bungling

handicraftsman skill with my kin-
dling genius to conceive? Is it not
I who suggested the whole plan for
the rebuilding of the city? Is it not
I who found Para mud and left it
marble? I will not quarrel with you,
but horses on that sea-wall or it shall
not be built.

*Alves.* They must be lions or I
refuse the business.

*Falcon.* You make me angry.
Horses!

*Alves.* Never, Señor. Lions!

*Falcon.* Be no more my friend.

*Alves.* We are enemies forever.

*Enter* OFFICER.

*Officer.* Which of you, Señores, is
Luis Alves?

*Alves.* That is my name.

*Officer.* I arrest you at the suit of
Señor Palacios.

*Alves.* Alas! must I lie in
prison?

*Officer.* At Señor Palacios' pleasure.

*Falcon.* What! arrest my friend, and in my house! Never! (*Throwing himself on the officer.*) Fly, Luis, fly! Feathered be your heels.

[*Exit* ALVES.

*Officer.* Help, there, without!

*Enter* SOLDIERS.

*Officer.* Seize this man. You shall pay for your outrage, Señor.

*Falcon.* Fate, thou art a plagiarist to poets. Shades of Tasso and Cervantes, I follow you to prison.

## SCENE II.

*Court-yard of the Prison.*

*Enter* **PADRE PACIFICO** *and* **LIEUTENANT ESPIRITU SANTOS DE LA TORRE.**

*Pacifico.* Cyprian, indeed! What does Cyprian know about religion? All he knows is how to go about doing good.

*Santos.* But, Padre.

*Pacifico.* Ay, I know your way. You will walk with me and talk with me, and use my spoon for your food and my bench for your bed, but the moment you have any interesting little peccadillo to confess, any of your immoral voyages and campaigns of Cupid, off you go to Cyprian. And why? Because he is stern and haggard, with flame in his eye and fury in his mien, and hates the transgressions of the flesh. He

33

preaches nothing but penance and purification. Now, I am altogether different. Had I the making of a new rubric, eating and drinking and the kisses of lovers should be the sole ceremonies of the church. What! do you think that because I am old and a priest I dream of nothing but martyrs frying on a gridiron and the unprofitable nothingness of cherubs? No, no, the visions that troubled San Antonio have no terrors for me. And wine! A glass of wine to me is as a flight of singing-birds with smooth carols. Yet you carry your confessions to Cyprian, and I don't listen to a decent sin once in a fortnight.

*Santos.* You mistake me, Padre.

*Pacifico.* Can Cyprian preach you a sermon, Señor? Are his panegyrics possible, his orations endurable, his funeral speeches fit? Does he know anything of the ordering of language

—language flowing as air, fixed as marble? Can he take seven indifferent words and by the mere conjunction or apposition of them so heighten their beauty that they shall show like moon-winged angels? Do you call his snort eloquence, his clumsiness elocution? Yet souls are committed to his charge.

*Santos.* Hear me, Padre.

*Pacifico.* Or is there anything deeper in him, anything hidden from ordinary apprehension? Nothing, or I lie. Can he resolve you the difference between First Cause and Final Cause? Can he argue you the question of universals, *universalia ante rem, universalia post rem, universalia in re?* Can he discuss wherein substance differs from matter and phenomena from things? Can he resolve you how an angel of God may twirl the earth on its thumbnail yet be able to dance with twenty

thousand of its fellows on the platform of a needle's point? No, not
for his life. Yet he has the custom
of the confessional.

*Santos.* Padre, Padre, faith I love
to listen to you, Padre. We men
of deeds, how words sway us! My
sword is my tongue. Well, well,
you say justly. I have been one of
them,—a dog, a very dog. There's
a little girl at Tabatinga could tell
you,—and faith a widow here in Para.
But that is nothing. On my word,
Padre, I do not go to Cyprian on
such matters. Cyprian is a great
physician, and he has herbs for all
hurts. I am not old, Padre. I was
only fifty seventeen years ago last
Easter, but the lustiness of my youth
begins to wane a little. The flood
is almost at the turn. Not that I
fail. Behold my legs,—saw you ever
such marble pillars?—and I have one
tooth, Padre, as sound as a coin.

But a multitude of little ills assail me. I am flushed. I am cold. I cannot sit, or stand, or lie down, or stay in the house or out of doors, or —or anything. So I go every two hours to Cyprian, and he feels my pulse and looks at my tongue, and prescribes for me. That is all, and, oh, Providence be praised, here he comes now. Cyprian, dear Cyprian, will you look at my tongue?

*Enter* PADRE CYPRIAN.

*Cyprian.* In a moment, Comandante. Pacifico!

*Pacifico.* My brother.

*Cyprian.* Know you that girl within?

*Pacifico.* I know of no girl, Cyprian; girlhood comes not within these gates.

*Cyprian.* She who lies before the cell of the last installed prisoner, the poet Falcon, and refuses to depart, know you her name?

4

*Santos.* Indeed, Cyprian, I think you mean the daughter of Titan Pape, the Cearense beggar. She came to me desiring admittance and detention. I refused. She said that Falcon had bought her for an arroba of tobacco. I could not make that a cause for her arrest. She said she belonged to Falcon, that she was the property of Falcon, that Falcon was her master, and a dozen such iterations of irresponsibility. I grew tired of her clamor and gave her admission.

*Pacifico.* And is she within?

*Cyprian.* Crouched at the door of Falcon's cell.

*Pacifico.* Spoke you with her?

*Cyprian.* I spoke, but she made no answer.

*Santos.* I'll warrant it. Her tongue belongs to Falcon, and she'll give none of it to another. But come, Padre, let us talk of something that

concerns us. My pulse is five beats
higher than when I saw you earlier
to-day. Do you think there is any
danger?

*Cyprian.* It may be. What did
you say her name was?

*Santos.* Erèrè.

*Cyprian.* Erèrè! Erèrè!

*Pacifico.* Cyprian, why do you start
and stride up and down distractedly,
and try that girl's name over in different tones as if to make it musical? You, a dreamer of impossible
divinities, a woman-hater by disillu-
sion!

*Cyprian.* Women were made angels,
and they themselves undo the crea-
tion. But this child! I cannot get
her eyes out of my head. She is
Truth itself. My soul recognizes
her. Stay you here while I walk
in the corridor awhile and cool my
thoughts.

*Santos.* Padre Cyprian, Padre Cyprian, wait until you prescribe for me! Shall I take the red medicine from the little vial or green decoction out of the great bottle, or keep on with alternate draughts from the two glass vessels?

*Cyprian.* Off, fool!

*Santos.* What!

*Cyprian.* Your medicine is all the same.

*Santos.* What!

*Cyprian.* Water differently colored.

*Santos.* What!

*Cyprian.* Away! I must be alone.

*Santos.* Oh, false friend! Oh, monstrous physician! And I deemed myself in process of a cure. Was my gout cured by fraud? my aching back straightened by perjury? Have all my fevers, intermittent, remittent, and continuous, been cured by tinctured water? Alas! they are not cured. I feel them leaping back on me one by one. Oh, my knees, my back! My head will burst! Help me, Pacifico. Rub my legs!

*Pacifico.* Cheer up, Comandante. This is only a trick of Cyprian's. You are cured, but he is vexed with you and would plague you with a dream of diseases.

*Santos.* Do you really think so?

*Pacifico.* I am sure of it. But did you note Cyprian's manner? Thought you what it means?

*Santos.* Indeed, I thought of nothing but myself.

*Pacifico.* He is in love.

*Santos.* In love! A priest in love! And with whom?

*Pacifico.* With Erèrè!

*Santos.* What! a great Cearense Leggar-girl?

*Pacifico.* With only half a chemise, and that in holes.

*Santos.* No shoes on her feet.

*Pacifico.* And his vows against it.

But indeed he has needed no vows until now. Water is not more indifferent to my throat than woman to Cyprian.

*Santos.* Why, he has it all to learn. I'll to him and give him a lesson. There was a little girl at Tabatinga loved me once.

*Pacifico.* Nay, if you come to that, there was a gray nun at Villa Bella——

*Santos.* Loved you!

*Pacifico.* And why not?

*Santos.* Nothing! Indeed, she must have loved much if she loved you.

*Pacifico.* Why, you spider's web——

*Santos.* Hush! Here come visitors.

*Enter* Pedro Palacios *and* Apparitio.

*Palacios.* Apparitio!

*Apparitio.* Señor!

*Palacios.* Did you despatch the

bills of lading for the seven cargoes to Portugal?

*Apparitio.* Yes, Señor.

*Palacios.* Did you see about the deeds for the five acres of land fronting on the plaza for my town house?

*Apparitio.* Yes, Señor.

*Palacios.* Did you tell Baron Maracajo that unless he appointed my cook's nephew as his private Secretary I would defeat him for the Presidency?

*Apparitio.* Yes, Señor.

*Santos.* Señores, may I ask your errand to this place?

*Palacios.* Go to my banker, Fereira, and tell him to buy me a steamboat for my guests to-morrow night. Bid Barboza, the publisher, be at my banquet. Get me a clean handkerchief, and buy me a hogshead of rose-water to dip it in. Why do you gape so, Señor Fool?

*Apparitio.* **To** know which of these things to perform first.

*Santos.* Señor, I demand to know why you enter here?

*Palacios.* Stay where you are, Apparitio. I can no more make use of you than I can of my shadow. What do you want, Sir Prison-plume.

*Santos.* I, Señor, am Lieutenant Espiritu Santos de la Torre, Comandante of this prison. How and why do you break into it?

*Palacios.* Señor Lieutenant Comandante, do you know who I am?

*Santos.* Not at all.

*Palacios.* Ah! Apparitio, speak.

*Apparitio.* **This** is Señor Pedro Palacios.

*Pacifico.* Señor Palacios, pardon Lieutenant Santos. He lives retired as it were from the world, and has not become acquainted with your virtues. I am more in the circle of civilization, and know the sun of that horizon. Only a few days ago I dared address you a little oration, an encomium, a panegyric on your merits.

*Palacios.* I don't want your encomiums, and panegyrics, and stuff. Thank God, I have got a tongue and can praise myself. Apparitio!

*Apparitio.* Yes, Señor.

*Palacios.* Have you the roll of my estate with you? 'Tis well. Listen, Master Comandante. You a lieutenant! Why, I will hire an army only for the pleasure of kicking lieutenants. Padre, you are a scholar of comprehension and can understand me. But there are some who think me only an ordinary man. So Apparitio bears with him a list of my deeds and dignities for the information of such vulgar minds. Read!

*Apparitio.* 'Tis a day's tedious business to recount them all.

*Palacios.* Never you mind; these

gentlemen can have nothing better
to employ them.

*Apparitio.* First, the estate at Monte
Alegre. Three mountains and a
forest which it takes the sun two
days to go around. Here are planta-
tions of rubber and cocoa and coffee.

*Palacios.* A mere trifle, but mark
you what follows.

*Apparitio.* Second, the island of
Santarem, thronged with wide-horned
cattle and haunted with innumerable
sheep.

*Palacios.* You are too cold, Apparitio! You read as 'twere a
catalogue of law cases. Put some
emphasis in the recital. Read as it
were your own.

*Apparitio.* Third, the Province of
Beni — terra-incognita — treasury of
untold fortunes.

*Palacios.* I hardly count this in
my present possessions. 'Tis for
my heirs, the Princes of the House

of Palacios. But skip this outer fringe of properties, Apparitio, and come to the heart of the thing.

*Apparitio.* The country-place at Olympos. A thousand acres of wooded heights and pastoral valleys. Sacred to sunlight and to birds. Armies of deer in the forest, and myriads of fish moving through their thin, devisible, diaphanous floors. In the midst of all the mansion, lofty and far-reaching, the bloom, the flower, the dream of generous living. Mountains of provender in the cellar and wine, rank on rank, in bins beyond perspective. Here Palacios rests.

*Palacios.* And I hope there are a thousand ways to be worse off. Read no more. Are you content, gentlemen?

*Pacifico.* Señor Palacios, we bow to you. Spoke you not of a banquet at your country-house?

*Palacios.* To-morrow, if the sun keep his promise to return.

*Pacifico.* You have made great preparation, I doubt not?

*Palacios.* No! A few thousand sheep and cattle sacrificed for the festa of my people. This in the open air. In my house a dozen or fifteen covers to be laid. The service of gold with jewelled cutlery. Simple, simple, simple!

*Pacifico.* But the repast, Señor. Most curious?

*Palacios.* Why, I had hoped for some little innovations. My people have orders to search the earth and sea and air for what is most unattainable. You will hardly recognize a mouthful in the meal. There will be some of that stuff the Israelites had in the desert.

*Pacifico.* And the wines?

*Palacios.* To tell you the truth, Padre, it is impossible to get wines that cost enough. Would I could dissolve diamonds into dew! But you are interested. Be my guest. And your friend here, the Comandante of cockatoos. I do not boast. He who eats proves. A dinner praises its giver. My poor house is at your disposition, gentlemen.

*Apparitio.* Oh, Padre, 'tis a part of heaven you are asked to.

*Pacifico.* No, no, Señor Majordomo, there you break your shins against theology. Your paradise at Olympos is doubtless excellently fashioned after the first pattern, as Señor Palacios here is fashioned after the first man, all virtue and magnanimity; but even so, heaven is a long ways off. I have a panegyric on heaven among my papers within. If you will wait, I'll fetch it out. What! you have no time to spare for heaven. Well, well, I'll come to your banquet.

*Palacios.* And you, Comandante?

*Santos.* If my health permits. But to-morrow evening is the time for the return of my remittent fever. Let me see. One, two, three, four, five, six, seven,—yes, seven days to-morrow at five o'clock. But hold! to-day, at four, my intermittent chill attacks me. My soul! I had nearly forgotten it. It comes, it comes! Pacifico, see how I shiver! I am going to pieces! Now, I burn! Will you not count my pulse? Cyprian, Cyprian, why do you desert me in my extremity? Gentlemen, will you see me die and not save me? Oh, will nobody look at my tongue? Cyprian!

[*Exit.*

*Palacios.* Do you think he will bite, Padre? I am glad he is gone. You and I can deal together more complacently. Do you know why I came here?

*Pacifico.* For some wise purpose I do not doubt.

*Palacios.* Hang your beggarly wisdom!. I can hire men to be wise for me for fifty milreis a month. A rich man should have fancies,—original, daring, great. He should make people stare and wonder, and never do anything that men of sense would think of. Now, this idea of mine. You could not match it in a century.

*Pacifico.* There is no use of cracking eggs after Columbus. What is your idea, Señor?

*Palacios.* Apparitio read it in a book. But that is nothing. I could have thought of it myself. You must know that to-morrow night I give a banquet to my betrothed bride, Jasmin Herrara. There will sit at my table all the millions and magnificence of Para. Parterres of rubies and rivulets of diamonds, and purses back of these as inexhaustible as fountains. But something will be lacking to our revel. There, where we are all rich, riches will seem a matter of course; where all are merry, joy will be a thing of no moment. This were monstrous. So I hit upon a device after the old pyramid-builders. I will clap a skeleton at our feast, so that the contrast may heighten our pleasure. Think of us, alive, fat, with fingers jingling our money, laughing at that pocketless and grinning guest. Is it not well thought, Padre?

*Pacifico.* 'Tis genius, Señor, pure genius.

*Palacios.* And hence my errand here. I desire you to let me have a skeleton.

*Pacifico.* But we have no skeletons.

*Palacios.* None in stock, none in stock. But you have malefactors, prisoners condemned to death. Have me one hanged immediately, and my surgeon will do the rest.

*Pacifico.* 'Tis impossible, Señor; there are no prisoners of such a grade here.

*Palacios.* Then hire me one to die. I will pay handsomely. Anything for my fancy. You would not care to undertake the business yourself.

*Pacifico.* Heaven forbid!

*Enter* PADRE CYPRIAN *and* TITAN PAPE.

But, behold, Señor, here is your man. Why, you old apostle of passivity, you apparition of a line, length without breadth, what do you want here?

*Cyprian.* He comes to talk with his daughter, Erèrè. Stay you here, Señor, and I will send her to you.

[*Exit.*

*Pacifico.* Señor Palacios, what think you of this figure for the appetizer to your banquet? Would he not

enact the part handsomely?   He is
poverty and death in one person.

*Palacios.* Fellow, I engage you for
my service.

*Titan Pape.* What is there to do?

*Palacios.* Nothing but to eat and
drink.   Follow me, fellow.   Apparitio!

*Apparitio.* Make way, all!   Room
for Palacios!

*Pacifico.* Adios, Señor.

*Palacios.* Go before me, Apparitio.
And you, beggar, stick to my heels.
Now advance.   Cry my name louder.

*Apparitio.* Palacios!   Pedro Palacios!   Make way!

*Enter* CYPRIAN *and* ERÈRÈ.

*Erèrè.* Hold!

*Palacios.* What!   Insolent girl, do
you detain me?

*Erèrè.* I care nothing at all for you,
Señor.   But my father, here, cannot
go with you.

*Palacios.* Not go with me! Are you mad? Why, he is mine by contract. Mine, not soul and body, but soul and shadow.

*Erèrè.* Yet he cannot go with you unless you pay my price for him.

*Palacios.* Beast, do you hear this? Will you be bullied from your own business by your daughter?

*Titan Pape.* In an ordinary case, Señor, I am at your service. But in a family matter——

*Palacios.* Oh, I will punish you!

*Titan Pape.* He who desires nothing has neither hopes nor fears and can be little hurt.

*Palacios.* Well, girl, you, what do you want? Apparitio, my purse.

*Erèrè.* No, Señor Palacios, it is not money. There is a gentleman imprisoned here at your suit. Grant me his release, and my father and I are your servants while we live.

*Palacios.* What gentleman is it?

*Erèrè.* Señor Falcon, my master.

*Palacios.* I know him not.

*Pacifico.* He was indeed arrested in lieu of Luis Alves, the sculptor, whom Falcon rescued from the officers and so earned his own imprisonment.

*Palacios.* What! my little sculptor. I only wanted him imprisoned so I could lay my hand on him for some work I need for my banquet. Why, yes, allow the other to depart. At the nuptials of Palacios the prisons must fly open.

*Erèrè.* I thank you, Señor.

*Cyprian.* I will give Falcon his liberty.                        [*Exit.*

*Palacios.* Now may we depart. Padre, live till I see you again. Remember my banquet. Eat nothing but salt until then. Now, Apparitio, spread your wings. Away!

[*Exit* PALACIOS, APPARITIO, *and* TITAN PAPE.

*Pacifico.* Fortune's ill-chosen mate

farewell. Stupidity still charms a world that graces cannot win.

*Enter* **FALCON.**

But here comes the other bucket of the well. Good-evening, gentle sir.

*Falcon.* Your blessing, Padre.

*Erèrè.* My duty and my greeting to my master.

*Falcon.* Gracious Erèrè, I am glad to see you.

*Pacifico.* You look melancholy, Señor. Cheer up. Do not let this brief confinement weigh on your spirits. Call hither the Muse, and she will give you the liberty of the world.

*Falcon.* Hard is the poet's trade. 'Tis but a confirmed, a continual duel with the world. He must confront this antagonist of adamant, give thrust for thrust, parry for parry, to the end. If he lower his point, 'tis death; if he retreat, 'tis

infamy.    Pace by pace with fault-
less sword-play must he push his
adversary till he fail and fall himself, for victory is impossible.    I am
tired, Padre, tired of the contest.

*Pacifico.* Well, Señor, why should
the world need any other diversion
than sermons?

*Falcon.* Padre, I will shift my
ground.    I am grown serious.    I
will cease to struggle with folly and
will fight sin.    I will inaugurate a
new religion.    I will sweep the old
superstitions away.

*Pacifico.* Why, I would not advise
you to be too serious, either.    Nobody is any the worse for a drinking-
song or a love-sonnet.    But you
speak of a new religion.

*Falcon.* Yes, Padre, I invented it
in my cell last night.    'Tis the only
hope of the world,—the religion of
humanity.

*Pacifico.* What is it to do?

*Falcon.* To reform the world. To make the rich good and the poor happy.

*Pacifico.* You deny miracles, and do them. How do you proceed?

*Falcon.* I will preach humility to men. Nobody shall desire anything that another has, and every one shall love himself less than his neighbor. There shall be no creeds, and all men shall be of one opinion. Wars shall be abolished, and I will lead a crusade to compel the world to accept my religion. There are more details which I will expound to you at your leisure. I burn to begin to save the world.

*Pacifico.* Alas, Señor, your religion is most exactly forestalled. It is eighteen centuries old, yet are there no doings such as you expect in a day.

*Falcon.* It cannot be, Padre. I am scrupulously original. The idea came to me in the dark vigil of my cell last night.

*Pacifico.* Why, know you not the faith whose unworthy priest I am? Humility is our basis, charity and love our buttresses. We desire men to know the light, and we persecute them if they turn from it. Have you anything new, then?

*Falcon.* Why have I not heard of these things before?

*Pacifico.* We disdain the ruin of the strife of man and provide refuges where lofty and humble souls may live in peace and contemplation.

*Falcon.* Do you so? Then I will forego my design. I will not change the religion of the world!

*Pacifico.* You will not?

*Falcon.* Nay, I swear it!

*Pacifico.* Noble youth!

*Falcon.* But in lieu, I demand that you admit me to your hospital of souls. I am wounded, and would leave the world. You need fear no hardships for me. Penance is my hope, and all I desire is flagellation. Dry bread is too good a diet for me, and a stone pillow, luxury.

*Pacifico.* I will have you entered of our order if you truly wish it.

*Falcon.* Sir, I was born a priest.

*Pacifico.* 'Tis a brief step, Señor, but a great distance. Think! You are alive, warm, vivid, musical, throbbing with hopes and exultations, and so you open a door and die.

*Falcon.* Padre, I will make my testament. Come here, Erèrè; lend me your shoulder for my tablets. So! Being in sound mind and about to renounce the world, I give and bequeath all my fortune thus: My wit to the rich, to be distributed at the next great mass, and the unnecessary surplus saved for another year. My courage to the poor, save that I do not think they need so mean an alm.   My poetry to woman, for as they are, for the most part, mere stuffed idols, 'twill be blood and blushes to their cheeks and Memnon music for their mouths. My love I leave to the hermit of the Andean woods, for him, I think, it cannot greatly hurt.   And so there's a philosopher of failure for you.

*Erèrè.* But do you leave me nothing, Señor?

*Falcon.* I leave you, but I leave you nothing.   'Tis a gift to take my discouragement from you, Erèrè. Fortune has better friends in store for you.

*Erèrè.* Fortune against my will, against my prayers!

*Falcon.* Well, Padre, come!   To seclusion, come!

*Cerita.* (*Without.*) Flores!   Brother Flores!

*Falcon.* 'Tis Cerita who calls. I must not answer. Farewell.

*Cerita.* (*Without.*) Flores! Flores! Lieutenant Santos! Let me in! I have a message for Señor Falcon.

*Falcon.* Cerita, what do you want?

*Cerita.* A letter, Flores, a letter! Oh, such a letter I am sure! I cannot give it to these walls. Let me in!

*Falcon.* Pray you, Padre, 'tis a poor sister of mine. Give her admittance. She cannot shake my purpose. Fate shall alter ere my adamant. But admit her, do!

*Pacifico.* Well, letters are—letters. It may be a summons to save a dying soul.  [*Exit.*

*Erèrè.* You would not stay for me, Señor, but a letter is more potent than flesh and blood.

*Falcon.* 'Tis from one of my creditors. I must leave the world honestly. But why doesn't the girl come?

Where does she think I learned patience?

*Enter* CERITA *and* PACIFICO.

The letter, the letter!

*Cerita.* Here, reverend father that is to be.   'Tis from Jasmin.

*Falcon.* Did you see her?  Read she my verses?  Does she love me? Speak!

*Erèrè.* Alas, poor me!  Master, farewell.  'Tis my turn to go away.

*Falcon.* No, child, stay with me. I need your help.  Oh, you should see this lady!  Her smile makes the world good.   Oh, her eyes, her hair!

*Erèrè.* I, too, have eyes and hair, Señor Falcon.

*Falcon.* Sweet, so you have, and a good heart with them.   But my letter, I forget my letter.   Come aside, Erèrè, and read it with me. (*Reads.*) "Señor Poet: I have never seen you, nor known you if I have, but you must know me, for your verses are very near what I have thought of myself. They say poetry is false, but I am sure there must be some truth in yours. If you would have me think it all true, be in my garden to-night. I will be alone in the house, and if I like you, I may credit you more than I do now.— Jasmin." What wit, what frankness, what simplicity! Say, Erèrè, is not all speech dull after such discourse as that?

*Erèrè.* Faith, 'tis as you say, for me.

*Pacifico.* Pardon me, Señor Falcon, but I heard the gossip of a name. Surely you do not intend to attempt Señorita Jasmin, the daughter of the rich Herrara?

*Falcon.* She whom I desire I will have if I have to wade through millions up to my neck.

*Erèrè.* And I will follow you though

you should set me to woo my enemy
Death for a bedfellow.·

*Falcon.* To-night, to-night! Why,
'tis five o'clock.  I must equip me
for this adventure.  But first, Erèrè,
to get you some disguise.  You cannot go about with me in that habit.
Padre, can you provide some garment?

*Pacifico.* My day of disguises is
done, but my heart welcomes such
enterprises.   Here, Erèrè, clothe
yourself in my robe and hood.  So!
Virtue itself would beg penances
from such a priest.

*Falcon.* Comrade,   away.  Love
comes in with the stars.  Padre,
adios.  Sister, get you home.

[*Exit* FALCON, CERITA, *and* ERÈRÈ.

*Pacifico.* It is wonderful what in-
dulgence I have for the laxity of
lovers.  Well, liberty is in the world
as well as law.  I will not make
myself a machine,—even a machine

of morality. 'Tis a sin, I suppose.
How Cyprian would reprove me!
A paragon of impossible integrity,
a man of iron, a fiend of virtue!
But here he comes. And how?
Sighing! Melancholy! Sad! Why,
Cyprian, what is wrong with you?

*Cyprian.* That which I dare not
say, that which I dare not think,
that which I dare not do, but that
which I am and for which I must be
damned eternally.

*Pacifico.* Oh, dear brother, what
mean you? Why do you walk about
so?

*Cyprian.* Walk! I would walk a
thousand miles if it would weary
down this pang. I have beaten my
flesh against stone walls, but the ill
inherits in every inch of me. I am
doomed!

*Pacifico.* Well, I know nothing at
all about men. This is all new to me.

*Cyprian.* Erèrè! Oh, Erèrè! how

could your benign beauty blast life so!

*Pacifico.* Èrèrè. Oh, I remember. 'Tis never so. Surely that girl has not bewitched you. You in love! Ice in love! Contempt and hatred in love! Oh! oh! oh!

*Cyprian.* Mock as you will. You do me good by mocking.

*Pacifico.* Why, you were the worst railer against womankind living.

*Cyprian.* Because I was the dearest lover of the excellence they should possess. An invisible apparition has hovered before me and lessoned me in perfection.

*Pacifico.* You were an idiot for your pains. Enthusiasm and irony are the two keys of life. One or the other you must use. Either see halos everywhere or know that there are nothing but bald heads like our own. You dower woman with your dreams which they know nothing about, being all realities. They are good enough. Not so good as you would have them nor so bad as you believe them. But now out of your scepticism and imagination you have built yourself a fine vision. What do you think she is whom you love?

*Cyprian.* Truth! No more, no less. Her beauty I care not for, but I have seen her soul. No winged thing nobler walks in Paradise. I can look upon her face and say, I love not her but God.

*Pacifico.* Well, then, would you stain her and yourself?

*Cyprian.* Heaven forbid! The struggle will kill me, but I will hide it to the end. Pacifico, my scars shall show only to you; but inwardly they bleed, they bleed!

*Pacifico.* Let us go in, dear Cyprian. You have herbs and I have words, and with such medicines we will try a cure. [*Exeunt.*

# SCENE III.

*Garden before* Señor Herrara's *house.*

*Enter* Falcon *and* Erèrè.

*Falcon.* Can you tune this guitar, girl?

*Erèrè.* No, Señor.

*Falcon.* Your voice could tune the spheres. Stand where you are. So! Now are the stars more eclipsed than when the moon does glide among them. These flowers forget their own perfume intoxicate with yours.

*Erèrè.* My dear master!

*Falcon.* A vision! nay, a goddess! Poets have fabled you before, and priests made religions of you, but now you are actual,—divinity turned flesh and dreams come true.

*Erèrè.* My heart will break with joy.

70

*Falcon.* If you are a goddess, be kind or be abandoned of your adorer; if you are a saint, do miracles or cease to have my prayers. Oh, Jasmin, Jasmin, make the distance between us disappear, for now we are the whole earth and the firmament of heaven apart!

*Erèrè.* Jasmin! do you speak of Jasmin?

*Falcon.* Why, yes, child! What do you mean?

*Erèrè.* And those things you spoke to me you did not speak of me?

*Falcon.* Certainly not! I was only practising my extempore orations to Señorita Jasmin. Jasmin, Jasmin, I take your name in vain, but you must forgive the profanation, for still do we swear by divinities! What! do you swoon, Erèrè?

*Erèrè.* Who,—I? No indeed. I felt a pain here, but 'tis nothing. I thought you were talking of me, and

I was offended. But, Señor Falcon, how have you come into such a sudden sickness of love for your new Jasmin, whom I think you have hardly seen?

*Falcon.* Frankly, my dear confessor, you must not think me too much in earnest. Love and poetry are both games of the imagination. We who practise either have a license for lying. We grow wild with words, intoxicate with tropes, mad with metaphors, and when in full fury we will swear that things are or are not until the heavens reel. You yourself, if you were given to loving, would become as eloquent as I. Suppose, now, you loved me, how would you go about telling your case?

*Erèrè.* Alas, Señor, I should need no poetry for that!

*Falcon.* But say you did.

*Erèrè.* Then I should say nothing, but serve you till I died, as I do now.

*Falcon.* Well, well, Erèrè, we are here in my love's garden. I sent you to spy out the country. What have you to report of the place? Is there not a noble charm of careless prodigality around us? Look at that fountain there, where half the Greek mythology is pretending to pour water out of stone vases. Or that tree clothed in vines like a hidalgo in a torn cloak. Why, this is the very seat of love and tranquil ease.

*Erèrè.* Señor, this place is as much out of elbows as my father's family. Here in front there is some grandeur of shabbiness, but behind the house all is pig-sties and stables. Sure your mistress does not live here?

*Falcon.* I hope I have made no mistake. Let me look at my index. Rosario, Flore, Santa, Felicite, Jasmin. Yes, yes! Rua Nazareth and La Paz. Here we are safe enough. And really, Erèrè, the garden is beautiful. I adore splendor, but I kneel to simplicity.

*Erèrè.* Well, if we are come to woo your lady, let us woo her. What is my part?

*Falcon.* Here, take this guitar. Fill in my pauses with what sounds you may. If you cannot make music, discords will do. Are you ready?

*Erèrè.* Ready,—not willing. But hold, Señor Falcon, your lady seems to anticipate you. Here she comes and more with her. Shall we wait to be discovered, or hide and hear?

*Falcon.* Quick, into this group of fan-palms. This is not my hour.

*Enter* SEÑOR HERRARA *and* SEÑORA HER-RARA, *dragging in* JASMIN.

*Señora Herrara.* Oh, you piece! Are all my sacrifices for nothing? Is it for this I have resigned all pleasures and held a seven years' famine of male society, so that I

might bring you up in virgin igno-
rance, a fit wife for the worst-minded
rich man in Para? And all the time
you have been reading novels, filling
your head with ideas of rapes and
seductions and all unnamable atroci-
ties. Oh, you, you, you infidel!

*Jasmin.* Why, mother, I am willing
to be good myself, but I must have
bad people to read about.

*Señora Herrara.* Oh, well enough.
When I was a girl we had no novels
to teach us such things. We had to
find out all about them for ourselves.

*Jasmin.* Oh, mother!

*Herrara.* What do you say, wife?

*Señora Herrara.* Say! say! I say I
am troubled with two trials, a husband and a daughter. What an un-
lucky woman I am! You are my
fault, but she is my misfortune.

*Herrara.* A fault! You were glad
enough to embrace once. Why do
you quarrel with me? Haven't I

made you rich? Haven't I made you distinguished?

*Señora Herrara.* You make me distinguished! Where did you get your distinction, pray?

*Herrara.* You know well enough that my grandfather was carriage-builder to the court. I am only three generations removed from being a gentleman.

*Señora Herrara.* Hark ye, Herrara. Your nobility reminds me of an old fable of the support of the earth. The globe is upheld by a giant, who rests on the back of an elephant, who in turn stands on a tortoise. Nobody in this town wants to go back of the tortoise. I could boast myself,—the Fereiras are not unknown,—but 'tis to no purpose. What is the use of a distinction you have to share with a thousand others? I have provided more nobly for our family. I have had the

Marquis Luna de Silva stand god-
father to our daughter. The King
of Spain is modern beside him.
When we go abroad under the banner
of his name we are sacred personages.

*Herrara.* Faith, you treat your
source of honor shabbily enough,
then. I just left him cleaning out
your cow-stable.

*Señora Herrara.* Well, the man is
simple. He doesn't know his own
value. There's no law against my
getting all I can out of him. 'Tis
such economy has made us rich,
which you claim for your own effort.

*Herrara.* What! will you deny
that, too?

*Señora Herrara.* Yes, and again.
You may have made some money,
but 'tis I have made you. I have
taught you how not to spend, and
therefore are we rich.

*Herrara.* Perhaps, wife, perhaps;
but I have always had the instinct of

getting other people's money, and therefore are we rich.

*Jasmin.* Indeed, if, therefore, you are both rich, why don't you give me some of your money? Never was a girl so used as I. I have to wear my nightgown indifferently abed and abroad. If I grow, 'tis nature's thanks, not yours, for you don't give me enough to eat to keep my little finger alive. I ask you for companions, and you give me the Marquis Luna de Silva, who was a mummy in the days of the first Pharaoh. I desire to go out into the air, and I am told I am too tender yet for the open climate. You keep me stalled in the house but to famish, not to fatten me. Do you want to start a new order of nuns, that you mortify my flesh for a symbol? Faith o' mine, if you don't let me out I will let somebody in who won't make a nun of me.

*Herrara.* It is all over, daughter. Your education is completed and you are provided for.

*Señora Herrara.* Child, child, when you have daughters you will know what I have done for you. How we mothers love our children to work for them so!

*Jasmin.* What do you mean? Why do you look at me so gravely? What is it?

*Herrara.* Well, child, it is marriage.

*Jasmin.* Oh, joy! Is it so, mother?

*Señora Herrara.* Yes, child, I have secured your eternal happiness.

*Jasmin.* But when is it to be?

*Herrara.* The betrothal banquet is to-morrow night, and the wedding as soon after as may be.

*Jasmin.* But oh, mother, I have no clothes.

*Señora Herrara.* Simplicity becomes you, my child.

*Jasmin.* I won't be married like a beggar, I warn you. But who is my husband, father? Who is the man?

*Herrara.* Shall we tell her, wife?

*Señora Herrara.* We ought to go down on our knees to pronounce his name. It is Señor Palacios, Jasmin, the richest man in Para, the richest man in the world.

*Jasmin.* Is he young? Is he handsome?

*Señora Herrara.* Young! handsome! What do you mean, Jasmin? The gentleman is rich.

*Jasmin.* And will I be rich, too? Then I'll eat dulces all day long. Can I have everything I want? Then I'll change my shift twice a week and not mend my old stockings.

*Señora Herrara.* Those things are nothing, child. You will have dresses, jewels, servants, equipages. You shall sit at home in as much state as a star and go abroad with as much circumstance as a comet. People will calculate nativities by you, and you will be a portent of prosperity or disaster.

*Jasmin.* All this for me! Oh, I will go mad for joy! Dance, father! kiss me, mother! Will my husband give me all this? Yes, and I'll have more, too. I'll have a new dowry every night before I go to bed. One night I will ask for a regiment of monkeys, and another for a tiara of diamonds. Oh, mother, a tiara of diamonds, a tiara of diamonds!

*Señora Herrara.* Your husband is a kind old gentleman, and will give you all you desire.

*Jasmin.* Old! How old is he?

*Señora Herrara.* About an age with your father.

*Jasmin.* Why, then, maybe he will die. Oh, father, to rise from the cold grave of matrimony into the rosy resurrection of widowhood!

To be free and to have wings! To be like the old Persian satraps and have Sardis for oil and Cyprus for wine and the whole unravished Cyclades for my bees to wing over! To be at ease and know the world creaks with burdens for me! To shut out the day and say to night, I banish you! To float over the necks of men like a goddess on a cloud! To be indifferent amid desire, languid where a thousand burn! And if one is not indifferent—why, widows do not need to blush. Oh, father, 'tis a heaven to marry a rich man from pure grace and have him die out of gratitude!

*Herrara.* When it comes to that, child, we will help you save your money.

*Jasmin.* Save! I'll have no more saving. I'll hire men to invent ways of spending money. I'll live a thousand lives in one.

*Señora Herrara.* **Well,** daughter, you must be married before you can be a widow, and that is what we are about to-night. **Where's** your god-father, the Marquis Luna de Silva? **Call** him here.

*Jasmin.* **Godfather,** godfather, one of your seventeen castles in Spain is on fire, and your twentieth ancestor has just tumbled from his horse in a tournament! **Come** hither out of your dream.

*Enter* MARQUIS LUNA DE SILVA.

*Silva.* **Do** you call me, child?

*Jasmin.* **Yes,** godfather, my mother attends you.

*Señora Herrara.* **Alas,** Marquis, dreaming in the open air under the stars! **'Tis** no way to make your fortune.

*Silva.* **Madam,** my estate of hope is in the past, and there I spend most of the time I dare take from your affairs.  But I trust I have not kept you waiting?

*Herrara.* Not a whit.  We wouldn't wait for you.

*Señora Herrara.* Be quiet, Herrara. No, Marquis.  I merely sent to acquaint you with our departure for this evening.  But have the pigs had their supper?

*Silva.* Yes, madam.

*Señora Herrara.* And you?

*Silva.* No, madam.

*Señora Herrara.*  How unfortunate!  The larder is locked, and Señor  Herrara  and  myself  are going  out  to  meet  my  brother on  affairs  of  Jasmin's  marriage. Could you manage until to-morrow? You shall make it up at breakfast. Or  there  is  a  banquet  at  Señor Palacios'  house  to-morrow  night. You  will  need  to  be  hungry  for that.

*Silva.* Alas, madam, I am hungry

now; but if you appeal to me as a gentleman——

*Herrara.* Gentleman! What is a gentleman?

*Silva.* A gentleman, Señor, is one who thinks all men his equals, and every woman his superior.

*Señora Herrara.* Do you hear that, Herrara? There's one in this house who knows my value. Thank you, Marquis, thank you.

*Silva.* I am proud to please you, madam.

*Herrara.* Pshaw! What is the use of such courtesies between people who know each other? I can be polite, too, when it pays.

*Señora Herrara.* Well, Marquis, we are going out, and must leave Jasmin in your charge. I will lock her up in the house and give you the keys.

*Jasmin.* Must I stay in the house by myself? Cannot my godfather be with me?

*Señora Herrara.* What! stay in the house alone with a man!

*Silva.* No, Jasmin, that would never do.

*Señora Herrara.* No, indeed! Marquis, you must walk around the house and guard Jasmin from intruders until we return.

*Silva.* But, Señora, the night is like to be cold, and I have no cloak.

*Señora Herrara.* One can always warm one's self by walking. Walk as much as you please, dear Marquis. But do not sit down, I beg you. I would not have you take cold for the world. Come, Jasmin, into your sanctuary. It is no use making faces. We have had too much pains raising you to let you be spoiled at the last moment. So, you are safe. Are you ready, Herrara? Adios, Marquis, adios.

[JASMIN *enters the house and exit*
SEÑOR *and* SEÑORA HERRARA.

*Silva.* Alas, an empty stomach has no gratitude. My soul recognizes its debt to this lady, but my stomach rebels. It keeps no record of the dinners of the past, it refuses to live on anniversaries. Why, this lady has rescued me from poverty, from dependence. Save for such slight services as one so incapable as I can render, I am free to do or dream as I desire. And yet I repine. Alas, 'tis not I, but this unfortunate appetite of mine. Have a care, Silva, or thy ignoble digestion will compromise thy nobility. Can I not be brave, modest, grateful, without the consent of my belly? Oh, I will set about my vigil. Hunger comes from emptiness, and emptiness is nothing; therefore hunger is nothing. [*Exit.*

*Falcon.* (*Coming forward.*) Well, I am amazed.

*Erère.* And I too, mightily.

*Falcon.* My admiration grew with every word she spoke.

*Erèrè.* What do you say?

*Falcon.* Such fire, such freshness! Moonlight and morning met together!

*Erèrè.* Is it possible?

*Falcon.* When we are married, Erèrè, I will have you about her person. You may from close acquaintance catch from her some of those graces that enrich her.

*Erèrè.* Oh, Señor, I thank you.

*Falcon.* Let me see if you have not profited already. Clasp your hands over your head and dance as she did when thinking of Palacios' death. Alas, you have not the gayety, the abandon.

*Erèrè.* I am not made for feigning, Señor. I am awkwardly true.

*Falcon.* No matter, no matter. But here comes our tethered Marquis. Into ambush again.

*Enter* MARQUIS LUNA DE SILVA, *reading.*

*Silva.* " Pyrrha, what, boy, all balm
      on roses now
Thee placid takes.  Thy simply
      braided brow
            Seems to him as these seas,
            Safe for some centuries."

Horace, thou break'st my heart.
Let me try again :

" How shall he shrink when storms
      and stars athwart
Threaten him ruin and wrecks fill
      his heart !
            And he does know thee strange
            Whom gold or planets change."

*Falcon.* (*Aside.*) Here's a translator
for you : turns a language of which he
is ignorant into a language which he
doesn't know.  I must speak to him.

*Erère.* Oh, Señor, are you here to
make love, or to busy yourself with
these idiocies ?

8*

*Falcon.* Love! Love is well enough, but this is an affair of verses. Señor! Señor!

*Silva.* Who speaks?

*Falcon.* Passing your gate, Señor, I caught—the ear of night being most open to such music—some lines, I thought, of Horace, admirably refitted to our tongue.

*Silva.* You flatter me, Señor. I am a mere bungler at this business.

*Falcon.* No indeed. I intrude on you, being also a worshipper of renown. Your translation is beyond doubt perfect, yet, if you will pardon me, there are a few phrases in the first, third, and fourth lines of the first stanza open to question. And the other stanza too, you could change that throughout.

*Silva.* I cannot see how. Your pardon, but I am walking in this garden for a purpose. If you will

keep step with me we may discuss
this matter.

[*Exit* SILVA *and* FALCON.

*Erèrè.* Oh, heart of mine, what do
I here? My madcap master leaves
me to keep tryst for him. Well,
the moon and I are punctual, but
there's no third person. Heigh-ho!
Is that a sigh or a summons? Indeed, this drowsy garden and the
trance-shedding moon almost make
me in love myself. There's nothing
for me to do but to sit down on this
bank and fancy some one wooing
me. Pray you, sit farther off, Señor.
No, I am not cold. This tree holds
me well enough. Alas, 'tis no use.
We girls cannot fill our arms with
phantoms as poets do. What noise
is that? Hallo! Jasmin at her
window. I am taken, or will my
disguise protect me?

*Jasmin.* Falcon, Señor Falcon!

*Erèrè.* Now, love or loyalty, which

of you is deepest in my heart? Shall I speak to her in my master's name? Woo her, win her for him and have his gratitude?

*Jasmin.* Do you not answer? Oh, I fear some stranger steals on my secrecy! I'll in again.

*Erèrè.* Stay, lady, stay!

*Jasmin.* Are you Señor Falcon? Answer, or I am gone.

*Erèrè.* Falcon! I am all Falcon. Falcon from head to foot, from heart to skin.

*Jasmin.* Well, then, why don't you praise me? I sent for you because you are the first soul who ever said a civil word to me in all my life, and now you turn stupid like the rest. Quick, tell me I am an angel, or I will throw something at you.

*Erèrè.* (*Aside.*) Heaven help me! I've forgotten all my master's fine speeches and there's no inspiration in the moon. I have a mind to run

away. No, I won't. She is only a
woman, and I will bully her into
bliss. Jasmin, (*aloud*) sweet Jasmin,
I do not come here to praise you, but
to possess you. I saw you, loved you
in the twinkling of an eye, and here
I am to have you. I am not worthy
of you—but I love you. I am horribly wicked—but I love you. If I
must come to confessions 'twere
death to me—but I love you. I am
lost in darkness and tumult, but the
star that governs your soul breaks
through my gloom to guide me—and
I love you. We are not equals, or
are equal opposites, yet queens must
be wooed by foreign powers, foes
have lief to kiss—and so I love you.
'Tis my only virtue that dares this
errand to you. I crave no alms, no
quarter, no reprieve. No fate can
make me flinch. Courage I have to
die, courage to live, courage to do
without you, courage to conquer

you. Stoop to me, then, fair star.
You shall show all the brighter
coupled with my shadow. And you
may find the soul that loves and does
not lie worthy even of your Paradise.

*Jasmin.* Oh, this is pure! This is
perfect! It wasn't for nothing that I
dreamed three nights running of the
bull in my father's pasture-field.
This is better than the Marquis Mi-
randa in " Damnation before Death,"
or the lover of Ardriel in " Kisses
of Fire." Oh, how could such luck
happen to me! Oh, sir! oh, dear
sir! oh, sweet sir! believe me, I am
your true slave. Don't mind my
rudeness a moment ago. I did not
know who you were. I will do anything at all you ask me. I will
marry you. I will run away with
you. I will jump right down out of
this window to you. Oh, how wonderful this is!

*Erèrè.* Heaven forbid. No, no, Señorita, not to-night. I am indeed under a vow not to run away with any woman to-night. 'Tis the birth-day of my saint, and I have religious scruples. But you love me, Jasmin? You love Falcon?

*Jasmin.* Why, I dote on you, Señor. Is all you say of yourself true?

*Erèrè.* How?

*Jasmin.* Are you so bad? Do you know all wickedness?

*Erèrè.* Alas, my past is darkness and the abyss.

*Jasmin.* Then I must love you. Oh, hark! footsteps approach. Some men are coming. Hide your-self.

*Erèrè.* Shall I stay and die for you?

*Jasmin.* No, do not die. Hide in the thicket until they are gone. I will close my casement.

[*Exit* JASMIN *and* ERÈRÈ.

*Enter* PALACIOS *and* APPARITIO.

*Palacios.* Apparitio!

*Apparitio.* Señor!

*Palacios.* Have you set the twenty French horns in the east shrubbery?

*Apparitio.* Yes, Señor.

*Palacios.* And hidden the fourteen trombones by the south wall?

*Apparitio.* They are placed, Señor.

*Palacios.* And strown the kettle-drums on the lawn beyond?

*Apparitio.* 'Tis done to your wish, Señor.

*Palacios.* And have you concerted with them all to burst forth at a sign?

*Apparitio.* I can wake or still them with a wink.

*Palacios.* 'Tis well.  Do you not wonder why I so besiege this house?

*Apparitio.* Why, no!  I think that when the music is at its desperate worst you will come forward and stop it, and so earn your lady's gratitude.

*Palacios.* Fool!  I would show her

how a king can woo. There are some fellows who would rely on their own merits,—a voice they have, or a leg, or some inward beauty; but none of that for me. I can afford some expense in my courtship, and if I cannot please my love with an army of musicians or send her presents enough to plead my cause, I'll leave mating to the paroquets and green love-birds.

*Apparitio.* Shall I signal the music to begin? But oh, Señor, you should open this diversion with some personal devotion of your own. Here is a guitar.

*Palacios.* Will it not be against my dignity? Truly, love turns us topsy-turvy. There is not a more peremptory man in Para than I am, but when I am in love I am a tame cat. Give me the guitar. I never studied these strings. Let me see. (*Sings.*)

There soars and sails a vulture,
And to his mates he calls.
Come hither, hither, hither,
To merry funerals.

*Apparitio.* Oh, Señor, that is not a fit song for a serenade.

*Palacios.* It shall be if I like. Do you think I will borrow the uses of beggarly minstrels. If I choose I will make it a custom for wives to be wooed with dirges, wedded with requiems, and buried to the tune of dance music.

*Apparitio.* You are always right, Señor.

*Palacios.* I will sing no more. I am better at orations. Give me room, Apparitio. I must have room for my gestures. Give me the whole garden.

*Apparitio.* But will you not have the orchestra play first?

*Palacios.* No! we'll have my speech

first and the music afterwards. What
does she want with music when she
can listen to me?

*Apparitio.* Nothing,—certainly.

*Palacios.* Jasmin, Señorita Jasmin!
Love-bird at your window, there!
Look forth! Do not miss this action
I present. Consider me! Note me
well. If the moon is not illumina-
tion enough, Apparitio shall get you
a lantern. Do you see anything in
me to object to? Is Pedro Palacios
the husband for you? The best of
me you cannot see. You do not
know what's within. 'Tis incredible
to myself sometimes. You will not
believe it, but I have no more education than a wild parrot, yet look what
I have done. I was born in a forgotten way, yet look where I am. I
have lacked everything, and I have
all. Myself has made myself.

*Erère.* (*Aside.*) Poor man! Nobody at all to blame for you. Well,

you don't know how to woo a girl. We are safe for you.

*Palacios.* Listen, my pigeon! I am a dozen dignities above the President of this Province, yet 'tis for you I am great. I have an empire for an estate, but 'tis for you I am rich. You should see the chamber I have furnished for you in my house at Olympos. Bedsteads of ebony, chairs of gold, mirrors of silver, chandeliers of diamonds, curtains of crimson, carpets of purple,—'tis a rainbow builded in a box, and all for you!

*Erèrè.* (*Aside.*) This is getting serious. She can never resist that room. I hear the creaking of a casement.

*Palacios.* As for jewels, my dove, you shall have seven sets of them, complete suits of armor. Besides which I have four wash-tubs full of unset gems, diamonds, rubies, pearls, in which you may bathe your feet.

*Erèrè.* (*Aside.*)  Oh, I must interfere.  Female flesh and blood can
never withstand such incantation as
that.  (*Coming forward.*)  Hallo!
Who are you who have followed me
to this garden?  Are you the boat-
men from the quay?  Oh, ay, mates,
wait for me outside.  No words, go!
Now for my serenade.  (*Sings.*)

All the air is dappled snow,
   And the moon's a whiter birth.
Moonlight and white roses now
   Are the hollows of the earth.
Sweet, awake, appear, and show
   These shadows what the light is
      worth.

*Palacios.* Impudent dog, who are
you?

*Erèrè.* I?  Who are you, too?
Have I made a mistake and given
my confidence to strangers?  But you
are gentlemen.  You will not betray
me.

*Palacios.* Villain, I will have you whipped.

*Erèrè.* What do you say? Twenty devils! I don't fear the two of you. Begone!

*Palacios.* I say, Apparitio, had you not better call one or two of my attendants here? This man looks dangerous.

*Apparitio.* Let me appease him. Señor, we only desire to know what you do here at this hour?

*Erèrè.* What do you do here yourselves? Answer me that.

*Apparitio.* Only a harmless serenade to a sweet lady.

*Erèrè.* What! do you serenade my love?

*Palacios.* You lie! 'tis my betrothed.

*Erèrè.* Impossible! she has no thoughts of marriage.

*Apparitio.* Let me call the lady up and she shall decide this question.

*Palacios.* Yes, let's put it to vote. This is an auspicious bridal eve. But I'll never doubt. What! that black beggar to compare with me!

*Apparitio.* Señorita Jasmin!

*Jasmin.* (*At window.*) What uproar disturbs the honorable quiet of this house? Señores, who are you, and what your purpose?

*Palacios.* I, Jasmin, am your betrothed husband.

*Jasmin.* Señor, I bow to you.

*Erèrè.* Do you not know me, lady?

*Jasmin.* I never saw you before· Come hither! Let me look at you more closely that I may know how to avoid you. Closer yet. (*Aside.*) Madcap, keep quiet till they are gone. (*Aloud.*) Away, Señor! I will know you again.

*Palacios.* Well, Señor, I hope you are satisfied.

*Erèrè.* 'Tis the wrong garden.

This comes of building gates alike. Adios.                           [*Exit.*

*Jasmin.* Señor Palacios, it does not become the modesty of my youth to seem to know you. My father and mother are not at home. If you love me I must be discreet for your sake, and tell you nothing that I might had I the warrant of their presence. Pray you, withdraw, and what the future has in store for me, believe me, I will choose with a grateful heart.

*Palacios.* Sweet child, I obey. Oh, Palacios, what a harvest of modesty and gentleness is ripening in this house for you! Come, Apparitio.

[*Exit* PALACIOS *and* APPARITIO.

*Re-enter* ERÈRÈ.

*Erèrè.* One word, dear saint.

*Jasmin.* I am too sleepy for anything but kisses. Can you reach up to me? See, I will kneel down and say my prayers on your lips. How soft they are! Oh, why do you fall back so soon?

*Erèrè.* More arrivals. Close your casement.

*Jasmin.* This can be nobody but the Emperor himself. Oh, Jasmin, Jasmin! what a miracle you must be! [*Exit.*

*Enter* MARQUIS LUNA DE SILVA *and* FALCON.

*Silva.* What noise is this? Jasmin! Jasmin! This door is safe, I will try the others. [*Exit.*

*Falcon.* Erèrè, is that you, my midnight Mercury?

*Erèrè.* You must take her kisses from my mouth, you must take her kisses from my mouth. I have them all caged there like a swarm of swallows in a chimney.

*Falcon.* What! have you spoken with Jasmin?

*Erèrè.* Ay, and sighed with her, and in your name.

*Falcon.* It is never true.   Is she in love with me?

*Erèrè.* Oh, most prodigiously!

*Falcon.* Well, 'tis a gift I have.

*Erèrè.* But 'tis no good.   Your prize is swept from you by a great three-decker of a man, a very squadron of a wooer.

*Falcon.* What do you say?

*Erèrè.* Palacios is to have her. What can you do against Palacios?

*Falcon.* Oh, monstrous!   Oh, impossible!   The laws of nature are against it.   He my rival!   His years, his infirmities, his villanies are rather my allies and plead against him.   But we will save her, Erèrè.   You will not let this happen?

*Erèrè.* Oh, I don't want to marry her, Señor Falcon.

*Falcon.* Let us go home and consider some plan to save her. She
must be saved.

*Erèrè.* Anything you please.
Anything you command. Oh, why
was I born into this vexatious world?

[*Exeunt.*

# SCENE IV.

*A room in* PALACIOS' *house.* PALACIOS *sleeping in a chair.*

*Palacios.* (*Waking.*) Oh, horrible!

*Enter* APPARITIO.

*Apparitio.* Did you call, Señor?

*Palacios.* Help, help! Is that you, Apparitio? Here, let me hold you. Ah, you are solid, you are real. Can you feel me?

*Apparitio.* Very plainly, Señor.

*Palacios.* Then 'twas nothing. 'Twas a bad dream. But are you sure I am alive?

*Apparitio.* I am certain, Señor. You are half choking me.

*Palacios.* Oh, it is too good! But can you feel these blows?

*Apparitio.* Señor, Señor! You will kill me!

*Palacios.* **Dog!** have you no gratitude that I am back with you? Oh, I have dreamed, I have dreamed!

*Apparitio.* In what manner, Señor?

*Palacios.* Apparitio, I dreamed I was a spider and spread my web and grew greater every moment. I wound my lines around the great earth and sucked the substance of it until it was only a dried shell. Then I drew a long thread out of my body and let it float in space, waving here and there until it touched the sun, when I darted over it and encompassed that orb with my filmy weaving. Then I advanced my lines in every direction and took in the stars, till my web was over the face of heaven and the constellations hung in it like dead flies. I danced up and down in exultation on my glittering bridges. I devoured the stars and I grew; I blotted the suns from heaven and was happy. One distant orb seemed left. I threw a thread across. It attached, and cautiously I crept over. Suddenly my bridge broke. I fell, fell, Apparitio, beyond death. I struggled, I sobbed, I sank, I died. I was nothing in an abyss of nothingness. Then I awoke. Oh, come here, Apparitio, and let me try my identity!

*Apparitio.* No, no, Señor! I give you my word of honor. There is no possibility of my being mistaken. I am black and blue with your resurrection.

*Palacios.* Apparitio, this dream is a warning to me. Why, even I can die. I must have more care for my health. Hire me a few doctors tomorrow. And, Apparitio, make a note that I dream no more.

*Apparitio.* Yes, Señor.

*Palacios.* This is an unjust world, Apparitio. Here I am richer than a king, mightier than a conqueror,

but to what purpose. My friends
envy me and my enemies have my
memory in charge. Why, there are
your beggarly soldiers who go up
and down the earth cutting throats,
and they are worshipped like divinities. There are your poets who starve
away into as thin a substance as their
songs, and their ghosts dictate to the
world. But nobody builds me bon-
fires unless I pay for them. Nobody
praises me unless by subscription.
When I raised the price of sugar
and took two million milreis out of
the market, nobody seemed to re-
joice. When I starved out the people
of Santarem and bought in their possessions for a song, nobody was any
the happier for it. I tell you, Apparitio, there has grown an ignoble
meanness in the world of late that
refuses honor to great qualities, and
I am the sufferer by it.

*Apparitio.* Ah, Señor, you may

soon scorn the world and its shifting tides of opinion anchored in Jasmin's arms.

*Palacios.* Ha, old boy! That's the note; that's the tune of my heart. Isn't she a creature? A spirit like champagne, flesh you could feast upon! But I say, Apparitio, have you made the preparations I desired for her reception?

*Apparitio.* All is arranged.

*Palacios.* Her first arrival on the island to be met imperial-wise! One hundred cannon to be discharged and twenty bands of music to volley forth in an instant!

*Apparitio.* 'Tis so ordered.

*Palacios.* Then the path to the house,—overhead a continuous bower of orange blooms, underneath a bed of roses!

*Apparitio.* Will you behold it, Señor?

*Palacios.* I don't lay much stress

on such natural adornments, but at the door some ceremony of salutation, some simple design of welcome. You have placed the statue of the river god at the entrance with his cornucopia so arranged that as Jasmin's foot touches the threshold there will gush forth a flood of jewels and gold pieces? At the same signal mechanical butterflies with wings made of thousand milreis notes to be released and flutter forth to entice pursuit?

*Apparitio.* The thing is done.

*Palacios.* Well, then, leave me to compose myself to some fit speech of reception.

*Apparitio.* Señor, there is one waiting without since daybreak. He is hungry-looking, and I would have sent him away but he claims to have come by appointment.

*Palacios.* What's his name?

*Apparitio.* Luis Alves.

*Palacios.* Oh, my little sculptor! Admit him.        [*Exit* APPARITIO.

I would to heaven I had more hair on my head, if only for twenty-four hours! But 'tis no matter. Jasmin loves my mind, and my person is good enough, after all. I wonder had I better wear my court suit or appear before her first as a simple gentleman and so gradually accustom her to my state? 'Tis time I was about it, or they will catch me in this dressing-gown and only four diamonds on each hand. Well, I'll go.

*Enter* LUIS ALVES.

*Alves.* Señor, I attend you.
*Palacios.* Are you a sculptor?
*Alves.* I am.
*Palacios.* Ah! I wanted an architect.
*Alves.* Señor, you have spoken the word. Only give me your purse and

I will build you another world! I
have invented seven new orders of
architecture. I will build you houses
that shall seem palaces and palaces
that shall be paradises. Oh, Señor,
be my patron, and I will make you
famous!

*Palacios.* Make me famous! This
creature is amusing. What do you
take me for? When I want art I
know where to buy it. I don't
meddle with home talents when the
markets of Paris are open to me.
All I desire of you is a little scheme
of decoration for my banquet-table
to-night. I will send you to my
cook, and you will confer with her
about the confections.

*Alves.* Alas, Señor, I am your
debtor, and must e'en degrade my
art to your pleasure. What is your
idea as to the piece?

*Palacios.* This: a sort of triumph-
phal procession of men on chariots,

on elephants, horseback, and afoot, to wind in and out of the covers on the table. The thing to be, as it were, a celebration of my greatness.

*Alves.* Whose figure, Señor, do you want in the chariots?

*Palacios.* Mine.

*Alves.* Whose on the elephants?

*Palacios.* Mine.

*Alves.* Whose on horseback? Whose on foot?

*Palacios.* Mine, always mine. 'Tis my triumph, and I'll have no intruders.

*Alves.* Well, Señor, will it please you to sit to me in different attitudes?

*Palacios.* Sit to you? Not at all. Where's your inspiration? Go dream me and draw me as you can. Quick! I hear guests coming. This way.                [*Exit* ALVES.

Heavens! they are here an hour ahead of preparation! My twenty footmen are not ready to receive them, and there's nothing in this dressing-gown to strike awe into a woman's heart. Oh, why did I not wear a wig?

*Enter* SEÑOR, SEÑORA, *and* SEÑORITA HERRARA *and* MARQUIS LUNA DE SILVA. APPARITIO.

*Apparitio.* Señor and Señora Herrara; Señorita Jasmin; the Marquis Luna de Silva.

*Señora Herrara.* Idiot! I told you to call the Marquis first. Let us go back and do it over again.

*Herrara.* What is the matter with you, wife? Here is Señor Palacios waiting to greet us.

*Señora Herrara.* My dear son-in-law, I am glad to see you. What a pretty little reception you gave us! The Marquis was much pleased with it. Let me present you to him? Marquis, this is the new member of

our family.   I am sure you will be
satisfied with him.

*Palacios.* (*Aside.*) There's two han-
dles to that jug.   (*Aloud.*) How do
you do?

*Silva.* Madam, your .wishes are a
law to my liking.   Señor, I am proud
to be your servant.

*Herrara.* There, thank heaven, the
politeness is done and we can be at
ease.   Shall we sit, Palacios, my boy?

*Palacios.* Yes, yes.   I was thinking of something else.   Damn this
dressing-gown!   Chairs, Apparitio.

*Señora Herrara.* A lover's absent-
mindedness is excusable.   Well, we
are weary and the chairs look very
—— Hold for your lives, all of you!

*Herrara.* Why, whatever do you
mean?   Is there any danger in the
chairs?

*Señora Herrara.* The Marquis is
standing.   Oh, be seated, Marquis.
Sit first.

*Palacios.* Why should he sit down before us?

*Señora Herrara.* His rank, Palacios. His sacred rank. Do, Marquis, I beg of you, sit down.

*Silva.* But, madam, it is impossible. How can I sit and ladies standing?

*Señora Herrara.* Ah, Marquis, you are too generous to so waive your rights. Since you desire it I will sit first. Jasmin, go over and place yourself by your godfather's knee. Let his words be religion to you.

*Palacios.* Well, madam, since this important affair is settled I presume we may proceed to minor matters. We are met, first to consider my settlement to Jasmin, and then to sign the betrothal papers.

*Herrara.* Ha! do you hear that, wife? The settlement, the settlement!

*Señora Herrara.* Do you speak of settlements? In a moment! Why,

Marquis, you have not put on your hat!

*Palacios.* Put on his hat!

*Señora Herrara.* Yes, the dear Marquis is so forgetful. See, he has it in his hand.

*Palacios.* Madam, madam, why should he put on his hat in this company?

*Señora Herrara.* He has the right to wear his hat in the presence of the King of Spain. I hope there is no one here will dispute his title. Cover yourself, dear Marquis.

*Silva.* Alas, madam, will you compel me to discourtesy to these noble persons?

*Señora Herrara.* Marquis, I yielded before, but in this I am inflexible. You must wear your hat or we cannot go on with the business. Son-in-law, beg him to put on his hat.

*Palacios.* Oh, put on your hat, put on your hat, put on your hat!

*Silva.* Madam, I obey you, but 'tis against my will.

*Señora Herrara.* Now we are comfortable I hope.  Spoke you of papers to sign and settlements?

*Herrara.* Yes, wife; you are grown dull to-day.

*Señora Herrara.* Perhaps I am dull and perhaps I am a foolish old woman, but a piece of musty parchment with the record of a thousand years is of more value in my eyes than a roomful of mortgages and milreis.

*Herrara.* You are talking nonsense, wife.  What is the good of a piece of parchment?  We don't use it even for writing deeds on any more.

*Señora Herrara.* Honor, Herrara, honor!  Marquis, tell him what a noble thing is honor.

*Silva.* If I could talk of honor, madam, I should not deem I possessed it.

*Señora Herrara.* Do you mark his proud modesty, Señor Palacios? Ah, this is what comes of having ancestors. Did you ever hear how the Marquisate came into our family? In the great wars between the powers of Castile and Arragon and the Moors the Count of Cordova, the Marquis's fourteenth forefather, did great service for the Spanish arms, yet he was so just that he was also beloved by many of the Moors; one of whom, the Sultan's father-in-law, intrusted to him a great mass of treasure for safe-keeping. So honorable was the Count that he would not touch an atom of this wealth, but turned it all over to the king, his master, who made him Marquis on the spot.

*Silva.* Madam, madam, you do me shame! What, my ancestor ennobled for a dishonorable deed! 'Twas not so. The king sent to demand the treasure and the Count refused it. Soldiers were sent to compel its surrender, but my ancestor, placing it a burden upon many mules, sallied forth with his followers and fought his way against his own comrades to the Moorish camp, where he delivered up the treasure to its owner. Then alone he sought the king, his master, to forfeit his life for the honor he had saved. But the king was as great as he, and forgave him and sought his friendship.

*Señora Herrara.* Marquis, permit me to know something. 'Tis a sensible tale as you tell it. What, enrich an enemy, a Moorish enemy!

*Herrara.* Yes, 'twere an act to mark a man a fool, not make him a Marquis. Any one who cannot look after his own interests is either mad or else one of those damned visionaries, and we know well enough what mercy they get in this world. Eh, Palacios?

*Palacios.* Señor Herrara, I listen to these things to please your wife. I take no interest in them, for I haven't yet begun to buy titles. When I do I will look at their teeth. But we are delaying business. Shall I read the list of properties I place in settlement on Jasmin?

*Señora Herrara.* Business, Señor Palacios! 'Tis a harsh word for us women. Come, Jasmin, let us leave the gentlemen to arrange these things.

*Jasmin.* Oh, mother, let me hear the list!

*Señora Herrara.* A childlike curiosity, Señor Palacios. You will excuse her. But, indeed, your recital of property would be foreign matter to her. She knows nothing of such things. Interrogate her on the virtues and accomplishments of girlhood and you will find her perfect. She has begun to play on five instruments, and she will paint you sheep in a landscape so that you will cry "baa." Then she knows history, and when you are melancholy she will entertain you with the names of the seventy-two battles in which the ancestors of the Marquis, her godfather, have taken part. But for business or money or things of that kind she has no talent. You might as well make cloth out of cobwebs as interest her in such matters.

*Palacios.* Oh, very well, madam. Are my gifts nothing? I tell you a queen's mouth might water at some of the items on this paper. I that am used to millions think them important.

*Señora Herrara.* Speaking of important things, Marquis, how came you to forget to wear to-day the great two-handed sword of your ancestor, the Crusader? 'Tis his only possession, Señor Palacios, but I know you would delight to see it.

*Palacios.* Swords; what have we to do with swords? Will you not let me read the dowry?

*Señora Herrara.* Dear son-in-law, we accept your dowry,—we will count it read. It must be no less than your wealth can deign to give or our honor to receive. Why should you be so passionate to spread this business out? Suppose I should catalogue our part of the bargain and force it down your throat. Suppose I should count up Jasmin's perfections, her youth, her beauty, her golden innocence. Suppose I should make a continual boast, as you have done, of the glory of her godfather's descent. Suppose I should recount to you the bead roll of his forefathers, as you do the items of your rent roll. What would you think of me? What would I think of myself?

*Herrara.* (*Aside.*) Wife, wife, you go too far! You will offend Señor Palacios. You will break the contract. You will mar our peace.

*Señora Herrara.* (*Aside.*) Peace! Peace, Herrara, is only got by arms. Would you have me lower mine and be under contempt? Not while I live. (*Aloud.*) **My** dear **Herrara,** let us walk in the garden for a while and leave these lovers together that they may grow acquainted. Come, Marquis. (*Aside.*) Marquis, stand you in the corridor, and enter if they grow silent together. I would not trust such a torch as Palacios and such inflammable stuff as Jasmin by themselves for the world.

*Silva.* What! must I cry "hem" in the corridor?

*Señora Herrara.* You must, you must! 'Tis for the honor of our family.   Come, gentlemen, to the air.

*Jasmin.* (*Running after her mother.*) Why, mother, must I stay alone with this gentleman?

*Señora* **Herrara.** You see, Señor Palacios, what a timid dove it is. Have you charms to tame it. Yes, child, stay.   Adios, son-in-law.

[*Exit* SEÑOR *and* SEÑORA HERRARA *and the* MARQUIS.

*Jasmin.* Did you speak, sir?

*Palacios.* I!  I don't know.  I am dizzy.  Am I standing up or am I sitting down?  Nothing is in its proper place, and the sun has taken to revolving around the earth again. Is that you, Jasmin?  Is your mother gone?—Well.  Is the Marquis gone? —Oh, well.  Sweet chick, do you hate me for being rich?

*Jasmin.* Faith o' mine, Señor Palacios, in spite of all my mother said I love you for it.  Have you really got diamonds, Señor, and will you give me new dresses?

*Palacios.* One for every kiss.

*Jasmin.* Oh, la, don't let's waste any time, then. I'd have some to my credit.

*Palacios.* Palacios, Palacios! this is as it were done after your own design!

*Enter* MARQUIS LUNA DE SILVA.

*Silva.* Jasmin, here is a rose your mother sent you from the garden.

*Jasmin.* Thank you, dear god-father.

*Palacios.* Thank you, dear god-father. Get me a rose, dear god-father?

*Silva.* In a moment, Señor. A word in your ear, Jasmin.

*Palacios.* (*Aside.*) Now they are whispering. This child seems frank-ness itself, but who can tell? She is as candid as sunlight, but who knows what's behind a woman's face? I'll test her on my old pictures here. For myself, I think they are damnably indecent, but the critics tell me they are as pure as an infant's dream. If they don't shock her I may know her mind is innocent. (*Aloud.*) Are you going, Marquis? What haste, Marquis? We are better for your company, Marquis.

*Silva.* Señorita, I kiss your feet. Adios, Señor.

*Palacios.* Take my arm, Jasmin, and let me show you my pictures. I have nothing but daubs as yet; nothing that costs above two hundred thousand milreis. What think you of them?

*Jasmin.* Oh, how beautiful! What is this? (*Reading.*) Ulysses parting from Calypso.

*Palacios.* Yes, that is how they pronounce it. But—hem!—do you notice nothing in the picture?

*Jasmin.* I! No. But then I know so little about art.

*Palacios.* 'Tis not art I complain of, but nature. Why,—hem!—they have no clothes.

*Jasmin.* Why should they, Señor? they are so beautiful.

*Palacios.* (*Aside.*) Palacios, I kiss my fingers to you. You are a made man. (*Aloud.*) Do you admire the figures?

*Jasmin.* Ulysses is so grand, with his great shoulders, his flowing hair, his straight limbs.

*Palacios.* Him with the brass hat? Why, what is he? I am sure I am that tall, and my chest, 'tis as great as his.

*Jasmin.* Oh, Señor, stand you side by side with him. Now I'll meas·ure you for comparison. I must take my apron to it.

*Enter* HERRARA, SEÑORA HERRARA, *and the* MARQUIS.

*Señora Herrara.* Hem! Jasmin!

*Jasmin.* Yes, mother.

*Señora Herrara.* You should see what a pretty little garden 'tis. Señor Palacios, I must praise your garden. There is almost everything one could desire in it. Of course we must not talk of the gardens of kings or noblemen, but in its way 'tis very well.

*Palacios.* You make me proud, madam.

*Señora Herrara.* No, indeed, son-in-law, there's no flattery. But I think, with your permission, we had best all retire to our apartments to prepare for the banquet to-night. Will you show us the way?

*Palacios.* I will send my servant. He will show you some little things perhaps. Some comfort, if no coats of arms. Apparitio!

*Enter* APPARITIO.

Apparitio, show my guests through this poor house. Show them the great stairway of the statues,—every one pure gold or silver with the cost honestly engraved on it. Show them the hall of mirrors, my favorite resort. Show them the great room of state with its pillars flashing with all precious stones, and the allegorical picture of my conquest of commerce on the ceiling. Show them—do not forget to show them, Apparitio—the modest little throne where I am used to sit and give laws to my servants. No pomp about the thing, but all the more an emblem of my authority. Then, Apparitio, take them through the ten conservatories of flowers, through the twenty bath-rooms of marble with flowing fountains, through the uncounted bedrooms hung in purple or crimson or gold;

take them on, Apparitio, until they tire, or until they have seen the few and insignificant trifles we have got here in Olympos.

*Señora Herrara.* Marquis, there is one thing contents me in this marriage. The riches of this house will serve to faintly remind you of the glories of your ancestral homes.

*Palacios.* Faintly remind him! Madam, one word. Is this gentleman, this Señor Marquis, to make his home with me after my marriage?

*Señora Herrara.* Oh, Señor Palacios, you would not separate Jasmin from her godfather! She has been used to the simple grandeur of the antique manners, and she would die if deprived of such society. Marquis, give Jasmin your arm. Here, Herrara. Let us explore these caverns of gold and silver.

[*Exit* SEÑOR *and* SEÑORA HERRARA, JASMIN, *and the* MARQUIS.

*Palacios.* **Are** they gone? Oh, can this too be a bad dream? Alas, no; the enemy is in the house. There is no escape. Oh, sit, Palacios, and dream again, for either way you are undone!

*Enter* FALCON *at the door.*

*Falcon.* Pedro Palacios!

*Palacios.* Who calls?

*Falcon.* Your judge, Palacios.

*Palacios.* Alas, what funeral figure is this?

*Falcon.* I come for appeal—for persuasion; but if these fail—beware! You cannot move me by your wealth, awe me with your power. You cannot buy my praise, you cannot bribe my disdain.

*Palacios.* This must be a person of importance. Will you sit, Señor, or shall I stand?

*Falcon.* Sit!

*Palacios.* Oh!

*Falcon.* I will be quiet though my injuries cry out. I will be calm though my hate convulses me. Anger seizes me at sight of your wine-dyed face, your flamboyant embonpoint, but I will be a model of moderation. Youth has the smooth, round limbs, age has the fringed yellow breeches to put on them. Youth has the white, level teeth, age has the turtle and dulces to employ them. Youth has the arms to hold a wife, age has the house to imprison her. Curses that this should be! Curses that I behold it!

*Palacios.* Do you speak to me, Señor?

*Falcon.* Is it you who have betrothed Jasmin Herrara? Is it you who have usurped the rights inviolate in me? or do you not know yourself? Then listen. I will not do you the disgrace of a mirror, but will draw you with a flattering brush. You have had the mercy of sixty years, and you have misused every one of them. You are short, and spread out on all sides like a tarantula. Your nose is like a talon, and your mouth droops at both corners like the tail feathers of two beaten gamecocks. In short, you are a satyr solemnized. And it is you who imagine to mate with that slender image of youth, Jasmin Herrara!

*Palacios.* Oh, this must be another bad dream!

*Falcon.* Is there anything in you to attract, to interest a woman? Are you a great devil or a great saint? Do you flit from flower to flower, from soul to soul, and fascinate women by the airy grace with which you ruin them? Honestly, you don't. Do you fold your arms in melancholy scorn and stand upright amid a world of crawling things? No; you grovel with the rest of the reptiles. To be plain with you, Señor, you are as commonplace a ruffian as ever bought a bride or sold a friend.

*Palacios.* Go away! Go away! If it is a dream, go away.

*Falcon.* But you are rich. I admit you are rich. What is't to be rich? Is it to own a great piece of the earth which is already gaping to own you? Is it to have a good meal and no appetite? Is it to bite for an apple and get ashes? Is it to have comfort and be without hope? Alas, riches are nothing. True greatness and distinction need them not. I am not rich, Señor.

*Palacios.* Mercy! My throat! I choke!

*Falcon.* Now that you are gentle, Señor, now that you are reasonable, I can talk with you and perhaps draw you to some settlement of our affairs. I have come in warrior

frankness to my enemy's house.
Magnanimously I have trusted myself to you. You must equal me
in courtesy. Here stand I, poor indeed, but with the adornment and
the prophecy of youth upon me.
Jasmin is near at hand, the full,
complete orb of girlhood. You will
look at us. You will say to yourself
that the making of beautiful mar-
riages is the sole real business of the
world. You will realize the hideous-
ness of your own desires. The marriage feast is prepared. The music
is ready. You will give Jasmin to
me and estate us with a great sum
for noble expenditure. This is your
mood. This is your meaning. Do
I not say true?

*Palacios.* Oh, just heavens! Your
name, your name, your name!

*Falcon.* Juan Flores Falcon, poet
and dreamer to his majesty the
world.

*Palacios.* Fiery devils support me! Is there no law, is there no religion, that I must suffer so? Is my house a den of cut-throats? Are my thousand servants helpless to save me? Señor, Señor, you shall be hanged to-day, and brought to life and tortured to-morrow! I will have you resurrected fifty times for my revenge.

*Falcon.* Why are you angry, Señor?

*Palacios.* Do you talk to me of poetry? Poetry! This chair is real, these clothes I have got on are real, my dinner is real, but poetry is not real. Poetry is a fool. Perdition to your poetry!

*Falcon.* Señor, this excitement is in exceeding bad taste. Since you meet my friendly advances so, I will leave you.

*Palacios.* Apparitio! Ho, there, Apparitio! You faithless fool, am

I to be at the mercy of wandering phantoms? Apparitio, I say!

*Enter* **APPARITIO.**

*Apparitio.* I attend you, Señor.

*Palacios.* Take this fellow and let him rot in my stables! Throw him into my cellar and let the rats eat him!

*Apparitio.* Gently, Señor. You will hurt yourself by this fit.

*Palacios.* I am old am I, and a satyr? You shall starve for that. I have no intellect, eh? You shall praise the witty writing of my whip upon your skin. I am not fit to mate with Jasmin,—Jasmin is for you. That is your death-sentence. Oh, you monstrous villain!

*Apparitio.* Calm yourself, Señor.

*Palacios.* Apparitio, I cannot trust myself. Take him where I cannot see him. To rob me of Jasmin, pretty Jasmin!

*Apparitio.* Let me help you to your room, Señor.

*Palacios.* Lend me your arm. I have had many a shock. Keep between me and that basilisk. Now I am stronger. Look you to him. Jasmin, my Jasmin! [*Exit.*

*Apparitio.* Señor, you see what you have done?

*Falcon.* Master echo, do you follow this man more directly than you do your own nose? Do you never think?

*Apparitio.* Alas, how should I? I have lived twenty years with Señor Palacios.

*Falcon.* Must I lie in his dens?

*Apparitio.* Are you not Señor Falcon, the poet?

*Falcon.* Some such thing.

*Apparitio.* Be comfortable, then, Señor. I understand my master. I have seen his rages before. I have known him in one of his sullen fits refuse meat more than seven times a day, yet, shortly, he would be doing kindnesses. He will forget all about you in twenty-four hours.

*Falcon.* You are a friend, Señor.

*Apparitio.* Only one who honors merit. You would not think it, but there is talent in this house. We write, Señor. There is a little coterie of us, cooks and waiting gentlemen, who are the best company in the world, for we praise each other's verses eternally.

*Falcon.* You interest me.

*Apparitio.* Yes. There is France-lina, the cook. She has the most marvellous vein of amorous poetry in the world. Her verses breathe Sappho and seductions. You—you'd think she was in love.

*Falcon.* Wonderful!

*Apparitio.* As for me, I choose a chaster line. My specialty is death, —death and damnation. Did you

see that little thing of mine in the
last number of the *Diario do Belem?*
It began thus:

O Death, O dearest Death,
Come suck my useless breath,
Make me again to be
A nothing like to thee,
Or chain me on the rocks
'Mid Hell's most hideous shocks,

And so forth, and so forth.  How
does that strike you?

*Falcon.* The and so forth is excellent.

*Apparitio.* Come dine with us,
Señor Falcon, and we will praise
your verses too.  And you shall eat
of every dish before it is sent up to
the banquet.

*Falcon.* Oh, lead me to the stables!

[*Exeunt.*

# SCENE V.

PALACIOS' *Banquet Hall.*

*At the table* PALACIOS, SEÑOR *and* SEÑORA HERRARA, JASMIN, SEÑOR BARBOZA, MARQUIS LUNA DE SILVA, PADRE CYPRIAN, PADRE PACIFICO, LIEUTENANT SANTOS, *and* TITAN PAPE.

*Palacios.* Has any one escaped my hospitality? Here we all are. I myself, you fellows as your rank may be, and lastly, the ladies. Well, have your stomachs got over the strangeness of this eating yet? Do you begin to understand how I live? I ask no thanks, but the man who doesn't get drunk is my enemy. Jasmin, I drink to you. I salute you in this cup.

*Señora Herrara.* Daughter, you should acknowledge the honor.

13       145

*Jasmin.* I'm sure I am much obliged to him for his trouble, but he keeps drinking to me so much I can't open my mouth for my own eating.

*Palacios.* But why are you all silent? why are you all solemn? The banquet is paid for. Where's your wit? Where's your laughter? Where's your reckless deviltry? Do your consciences permit you to deal this way with me? I don't expect you to be as amusing as I am, but in your way, in your way. Titan Pape, I hired you to be melancholy, but there's more need of mirth. Laugh, then, talk and laugh.

*Titan Pape.* Talking and laughing were not included in my contract, Señor.

*Señora Herrara.* You are right, son-in-law, to demand conversation. What are these viands to wit? What

is this wine to sentiment? I declare
in my house we often become so rapt
in the Marquis Luna de Silva's talk
and legends of the past that we forgot to use food at all. Marquis, you
are the man to open this debate. A
person of your consequence is never
at a loss for conversation. Pray, say
something.

*Silva.* Certainly, madam. Will
you pass me that truffled fowl?

*Señora Herrara.* Always witty,
Marquis. Now you, lieutenant.
Soldiers fear nothing, and your
tongues are as bright as your swords.

*Santos.* Madam, have you any diseases?

*Señora Herrara.* Mercy! Do you
insult me, man?

*Santos.* Alas, you bade me speak!
What is there to talk about in the
world but the prospect of leaving it.
I cannot open my eyes but I see such
a mass of diseases, such a sum of

sickness, that my senses reel. You, madam, have a healthy color, but I have known people of your complexion, and they were corpses before night.

*Señora Herrara.* Just Heaven, I have cried the wrong tiger! Ah, Señor Barboza! You, who dwell amid poetry and live off of eloquence, you can help us in our need.

*Barboza.* Madam, I sell words, not throw them away.

*Señora Herrara.* Had I your economy, I'd buy the universe. Padre Pacifico, I throw *tres seizes* when I call on you. Your profession is in your tongue.

*Pacifico.* Alas, madam, I cannot talk in this off-hand, hasty way. Give me time, two or three days or a month, and I will concoct you as pretty a conversation as you would wish. Or I have something in my pocket that may serve. 'Tis my choicest prose, a funeral oration on one of the brothers of our order at the Breves Mission. Will you hear it?

*Palacios.* Funerals! who talks of funerals? This is my betrothal banquet. What's the matter with this menagerie, any how? Do you want more wine to stir you up? Is there no blood in any of you? Of course we can't have real wit, stories that will make us roar, until the ladies go. But do none of you men know a rhyme of gibberish or tricks to blacken one another's faces? If you break a plate or two for a jest, I'll never cry. Damn dulness, I say! I drink to you, Jasmin.

*Cyprian.* (*Starting up.*) What face was that at the door-way?

*Titan Pape.* 'Twas my daughter, I think, Erèrè.

*Cyprian.* Señor, you must excuse me. Ladies, I crave your pardon.

13*

My head is dizzy, I must out into the air.      [*Exit.*

*Pacifico.* Let no one be disturbed. This is a fainting sickness that comes upon my brother often and unexpectedly.

*Santos.* Perhaps it is catching. Oh, Señor Palacios, send for a doctor! I saw Cyprian turn yellow, and 'tis a sign of the plague. Quick! Would you have us all lying stiff beside your table?

*Palacios.* Pooh! You a soldier! The Padre is only suffering from a repletion of emptiness. He ate nothing. But, oh, gentlemen, I beg of you to be merrier! This is my banquet, and if nobody laughs I am disgraced. What do you want, Apparitio? Don't annoy me when I am enjoying myself.

*Apparitio.* There's a girl at the door and she sends a message to you.

*Palacios.* Who's she? I know no

girls but Jasmin. Sweet Jasmin, I drink to you.

*Apparitio.* She says that if you want entertainment for your banquet, Falcon, the poet, whom you have locked in the stable, will furnish it. She says he is a great magician and can do miracles.

*Palacios.* What! is he a juggler too? I thought he was nothing but a poet. If he has any real talents, if he can swallow fire or stand on his head on a pyramid of decanters, we'll have him in. Hey, lads?

*Omnes.* We'll have him in!

*Palacios.* Let him loose, Apparitio. Who's afraid? [*Exit* APPARITIO.

Where's any one will do for his guests what I do? They say I'm proud, but I keep up no dignity to those I favor. Jasmin, your health. I might eat by myself, drink by myself, be married by myself, and no thanks to any of you, but I am

lovable and full of sweet society.
There's no tyranny in me, but every
man in his place I say.  Whoop!

*Enter* FALCON, *bursting in without coat and
the straw sticking to him.*

Here's our man.  Now we shall
laugh.  To it, Señor.  Say something witty to begin with.

*Falcon.* What is this place, these
people?  The lights dazzle me!

*Omnes.* Ha! ha! ha!

*Falcon.* Oh, Señor, I know you!
You are my Host of the Stables.
How shall I pay for my entertain-
ment?

*Omnes.* Ha! ha! ha!

*Falcon.* What! do you all laugh
at me?  Which shall I kill first?

*Omnes.* Ha! ha! ha!

*Falcon.* Alas, pitiable me!  Jasmin is here.  I am lost in her
sight.

*Palacios.* Do you call this fooling?

Where's your tricks? Erèrè told us you were a magician.

*Falcon.* Erèrè!

*Palacios.* Swore you could do miracles.

*Falcon.* Said she so! Then I can. Pardon me, all of you. My entrance was only a stage feint. Now to my conjuration. But first, will you assist me, will you help me in my act?

*Palacios.* Ay, old boy, till we smell sulphur.

*Falcon.* Then I must be among you. This seat beside you, Señorita, will do. (*Aside.*) Jasmin, I love you, I adore you!

*Jasmin.* (*Aside.*) Well, you may, sir, but not before Señor Palacios.

*Palacios.* What are you whispering there?

*Falcon.* Only an incantation to my familiar spirit. Now, are you ready, Señores? You are to watch me, to follow my every motion, match each of my gestures, till your very thoughts grow one with mine. Behold, I pour out a glass of wine. Do you the same. Now, to my lips. And you. Off with it!

*Palacios.* That's easy enough. But what's the virtue of it?

*Falcon.* Do not be impatient, Señor. Impatience will spoil all. The spell will work soon enough. Again I pour out wine, again you follow me.

*Palacios.* But what is it for? Is it fortune-telling or raising a black spirit in a circle?

*Falcon.* 'Tis not for you to know yet. I make fortunes, not tell them. Again, ready?

*Palacios.* Faith, I feel a dizziness in my head. Is that where the spell work first?

*Herrara.* I think it rather enters at the knees.

*Palacios.* Whoop! Now the table

begins to turn. Draw back or the comet will singe you.

*Falcon.* Hush! The sacred fumes arise. The moment is propitious. But one influence works against me. There's one thing to be done yet.

*Palacios.* What's one thing? You lie, there's two things, three things up and down before me.

*Falcon.* The ladies must leave the room. The secret spell will not work with the ladies present.

*Señora Herrara.* Secret, indeed! I don't believe you have any secret.

*Herrara.* I beg you, wife. Maybe he has and maybe he hasn't. It don't cost anything to try. He spoke of making our fortunes.

*Palacios.* Ha! ha! What's the use of secrets and ladies in the room? You must go, ladies. I'll help you out if I can feel where you are. Which is my hand and which is the door?

*Falcon.* Sit still, Señor Palacios, and I'll help the ladies out. Come, Señoritas. Dear madam, farewell. Jasmin (*aside*), in an hour from now in the garden. By the gods I love you! Adios! Adios!

*Palacios.* What a man he is! Ladies or the bottle, it's all one to him.

*Falcon.* Now to the test.

*Herrara.* If it's gold or silver, I have some acid in my pocket.

*Falcon.* Peace, sordid soul! 'Tis a greater matter than that. Know you that by my enchantment I can for one night command the treasures of the world. Obey me, follow my orders, and to-night you may live as lords of nature and of dreams. But first, the sacred wine again. Drink slowly. Now I am prepared. I dilate with power. Señor Palacios, what is't you want?

*Palacios.* Want! What do you

mean by want? I want for nothing. There's wine in the cellar.

*Falcon.* But what do you desire? You may choose and have.

*Palacios.* Apparitio, what do I desire? Where's Apparitio?

*Falcon.* Apparitio cannot help you. 'Tis the secret inclination of your soul I grant.

*Palacios.* What are you preaching about souls for? Gentlemen, and you be so moral I'll sleep. Is there no music in you? Have you no risky songs, no indecent ballads? (*Sings.*)

There was a lass went out to swim;
　All in the summer weather;
Alone she went, alone she came,
　Yet two came home together.

Where's Jasmin? That's what I want! Jasmin and a boy heir. Let him have my nose and a pock-marked face, and be born with a caul. Can

14

you do it, Wizard?   We'll have a
christening to-night.   Drink to my
boy heir, all of you.   Can you not
stand up to drink to my boy heir?

*Falcon.* Señor, it shall be done.
Now, Herrara, what for you?

*Herrara.* Faith, I dare not say it
aloud.   If my legs will bear me, I'll
come around and speak it in your
ear.

*Falcon.* Take my hand.   So!   Is
that all?   You shall live forever—
to-night.   Padre Pacifico, speak!

*Pacifico.* I desire nothing but to
be a bishop and preach twice a week
in the great cathedral.   If you have
any power, do not judge me by ap-
pearances.   I am not drunk, Señor.
'Tis against the policy of our order
to get drunk.   I am only melancholy.
There was a lady loved me once, and
'tis thinking of her makes me cry
thus.   But I am not drunk.   Do not
injure me in your thought, Señor.

*Falcon.* You shall not need to cry —to-night. Lieutenant Santos, shall I kill Death for you—to-night.

*Santos.* Death! Who fears death? Not I. If my sword were here I'd show you. Do you look black at me, Señor, or you? My blood boils in me. What's the matter with this chair? It's legs won't walk.

*Falcon.* Enough! Enough! Look at me, Señor Palacios. I will take you out into Arcadia. You shall lie on green couches under the silver trees. To-night, to-night we shall roam at large like gods.

*Palacios.* Yes, let's be gods.

*Falcon.* But, Señor, before we enter into this domain you must disinherit yourself of your estate— deny yourself authority. In Arcadia we must all be equal. You shall be Pan, keeper of the woods, and we shall be visitant divinities.

*Palacios.* Yes, I know I am Pan.

Gentlemen, I command you to be my equals.

*Falcon.* Call in Apparitio, Señor, and resign your keys and command to him. Apparitio!

*Palacios.* Who's Apparitio? (*Enter* APPARITIO.) What do you want?

*Falcon.* He forgets his shadow. Señor, give over the order of the house to him.

*Palacios.* Apparitio, you are a free man. Here's my keys. You are my equal, and are to go into Arcadia to wait on me.

*Falcon.* Oh, joy! Rise, wake, all of you! Our voyage to Arcadia begins. What a company!

*Herrara.* Faith, I cannot see. A candle, a candle!

*Barboza.* Is't bedtime?

*Santos.* Where am I?

*Falcon.* Rise, noble gentlemen. Stand in line. Dress company! Let your courage be your support, and leave off holding by your chairs. Ready! Attention! March! Follow me!

*Palacios.* Follow me, I say! Let somebody tie this floor down.

*Pacifico.* Oh, if I should fall! There's an abyss on each side of me.

*Falcon.* Now, Señores, dance!

*Palacios.* This is excellent. What steps I can make!

*Herrara.* My blood is up too.

*Falcon.* Faster, higher!

*Palacios.* Titan Pape, why the devil don't you hop higher?

*Falcon.* Now we are off!

*Palacios.* Now we are off!

[FALCON *pipes on a fork, and dances fantastically about the room followed by the rest.*

*Falcon.* Thrice about the room I go,
Pipe and crack my cheeks and blow,
Thrice the banquet board about,

Followed by this rabble rout.
Ah, you fawn on me athirst,
Swilling wind until you burst,
Fools of life, whom I can make
Fools of fancy though awake.
On your eyelids lies my charm,
To your hearts you hug my harm;
Truth I bring, but Truth becomes
Poison in ignoble homes.
Though your real selves of the past
By my spell is overcast,
Still yon glimpse through doors I
    ope
Every one his secret hope.
You (*to* PALACIOS) would seek un-
    rivalled rule;
You (*to* HERRARA) would make the
    world your fool;
You (*to* BARBOZA) would seem un-
    seemly wise;
You (*to* PACIFICO) would have a bene-
    fice;
Ill it were to all the rest
If a single dream were blest.

All the wealth that men might hold,
The Hesperidean gold,
Nothing is to you, for you
Never could believe it true.
See, above the moon does glide
Like an unashamed bride,
And the stars triumphant kill
Every ghost and gliding ill;—
All your treasure's in your eyes!
Make or mar your Paradise!
Halt! My spell is wrought and
    done:
You are free to walk or run.
Out, my sottish, goblin crew
And the golden years renew.
Twenty minutes I do give
In Arcadia you to live,
Ere your warring tempers will
All the place with clamor fill.
I have brought you to the gates,
Go, go, go, and try your fates.

Away! away! Into Arcadia, all of
you. *[Exeunt.*

# SCENE VI.

PALACIOS' *garden.*

*Enter* PALACIOS *and* JASMIN.

*Jasmin.* Does the freshness of the air revive you, Señor?

*Palacios.* I know your sweet hand and I know your face. You are Jasmin, and this is my garden. What makes my voice so thick? Are you deaf? Oh, let me sit on this bank and put my feet in your lap!

*Jasmin.* This is not your garden, Señor! This is Arcadia. You are to play a part here,—one Pan, a hairy fellow with an ear for music.

*Palacios.* This is my garden. I am not Pan, I am Pedro Palacios. But if you take my property away from me I am nobody. This domain

164

is me, and the money at my banker's
is another me.

*Jasmin.* How sweet you are, then,
Señor Palacios! The air of this
place is fragrant and haunted with
the souls of flowers.

*Palacios.* The air of this garden is
a private, a special air. The place is
walled from the common part of my
estate. There are fourteen acres of
stars attached to it and constellations
not public to the world.

*Jasmin.* And you have made it all
over for an Arcadia. How kind,
Señor!

*Palacios.* You mock me with making over. I tell you this garden
belongs to me. That house belongs
to me. You belong to me. Everything belongs to me.

*Jasmin.* Alas, no, Señor. Not to-
night. Girls belong to anybody in
Arcadia. Señor Falcon has made a
new law.

*Palacios.* Falcon! Now I remember. Marquis Luna de Silva! Now I know all. Let me away! Let me arouse my people! There's death in my mind. Oh, I am bloody-thoughted!

*Enter* APPARITIO *and* TITAN PAPE.

*Apparitio.* Hey, old skeleton, canst drink? Will your bones hold moisture? Stand steady, I say! Oh, do not let me break! You'd not believe it, old mouse-trap, but I was never drunk before. What noise was that? Do you think I am afraid? Here's my heart thundering in my breast. I am free. I can laugh, I can frown. If my master were here I'd frown on him. Master, do I say? There's no masters more. Down on your knees to me, you villain!

*Titan Pape.* Alas, what happiness I have lost! I cannot get drunk.

*Apparitio.* Titan Pape, I'll show

you how to be a gentleman. I learned
it of my master. Now! Señor Fool,
get me my shaving-cup! Idiot, buy
me a province before breakfast! Apparitio, dear Apparitio, I have the
toothache. And so forth. Oh,
Lord, how easy it is to be a gentleman when other people will let you!

*Palacios.* (*Advancing.*) **Dog!** do
you mock me?

*Apparitio.* **Dog** yourself. I am
free. I can fly. Will you frown at
me out of your cloudy windows?
Then I'll beat you. (*Seizes* PALA-
CIOS.) Titan Pape, help me to beat
him.

*Titan Pape.* I'll not help you beat
him, but I'll keep him from objecting.
Gently, Señor; no striking back.

*Palacios.* Oh, murder, villains,
murder! Help me, Jasmin!

[*Exit* PALACIOS, APPARITIO, *and*
TITAN PAPE.

*Jasmin.* Why should the poor, dear

gentleman be beaten? I have not married him yet. But look! Here comes my other betrothed, and my father with him. I must not see Falcon in such company. There's plenty of privacy about.   [*Exit.*

*Enter* FALCON *and* HERRARA.

*Herrara.* No, Señor, I care nothing for these gewgaws of entertainment and display. My money is set to better uses. It waxes, not wastes. Those who come after me will find me fat, I assure you.

*Falcon.* Those who come after you are worms. You'll scarce content them.

*Herrara.* Worms! You are plain, Señor. Then I'll pay you in kind. I like you well enough, but there's some people who do not want you for an every-day diet. That jest you played on us was good. You led us by the nose,—you made us

see signs and wonders. I can laugh
at it; but Palacios is dreadful in his
anger. You are witty, but where
wealth is, wit were best away. Go
away and play jokes on somebody
else and we will laugh at them.
And this girl who follows at your
heels; let her go with you. I
would not have my daughter meet
her in this garden for the world.
The innocent must be protected,
Señor.

*Falcon.* Señor, I can advise myself. And I can protect this child,
even from your daughter.

*Herrara.* I will not fight! I will
not fight! I have said all. Adios.

[*Exit.*

*Erèrè.* Must we go away, Señor
Falcon?

*Falcon.* Erèrè, I am a top whirled
by chance. I shall never know
which way I really point until I fall
dead. What do you advise?

15

*Erèrè.* Oh, Señor, now is your hour and opportunity! The master of the house is drunk, the guests dispersed, the servants lost in liberty and these obscure woods. Make your play. Seek out Jasmin, besiege her with prayers, draw her to the river where the boats await. I will secure Padre Pacifico to fly with us, and to-night shall this heaven lose its goddess and the little hut in Para be enriched with golden guests. Is it not well told?

*Falcon.* A pretty telling of a pretty dream. Have you more of it?

*Erèrè.* Dream! You are dull to-night. Oh, let your heart be fire, your hand be iron, your tongue be honey, and nothing can resist you! Bolts and bars cannot resist you. Your love must come, inevitably she must come to you. Tides are not surer. Oh, were I a man!

*Falcon.* Heaven keep us from ca-

lamities! But what would you do
if you were a man?

*Erèrè.* Make wings spring from
Jasmin's shoulders to fly to me.
Make her blood turn to quicksilver
to run to me. Master of mine, you
need only to dare and all is won.
Fortune and love hunt not a flying
suitor.

*Falcon.* She is a sweet lady, but I
fear her fortune is above me.

*Erèrè.* You are a fool! Sweet
lady, and hold back! Fortune, and
hesitate! If she is a goddess, she
has only got two arms. If she owns
the earth, she can only sleep in one
bed at once. But see! There she
walks in the garden, like a flower
whose head droops, wanting the
strength of the sun. Now she stands
irresolute and waiting. Are you
dead? Go to her! Wake her!
Win her! But no! In this mood
I had as well send an icicle to woo

a rose-bud to open.  Hide you here and I'll be your messenger.

[*Exit* FALCON.

*Enter* JASMIN.

Jasmin, dear lady!

*Jasmin.*  Is that you, Erèrè?

*Erèrè.*  Dear Jasmin, can you keep here so quiet when my master is scouring the wood hungry for your love?  I left him by the Fountain of the Naiads, but now almost mad with the pain of not finding you. Hark!  Is that his cry?  Ah, no! 'tis only the ringing of the anvil bird.  Unless you take this instant opportunity and elope with Señor Falcon from this place, I fear he cannot live through the night.  Shall I bring him here?  Or better, let us walk towards him,—'tis the path to liberty.

*Jasmin.*  No! no! no!  I can't elope with so little ceremony as this.

And besides, I have not made up my mind to love Señor Falcon.

*Erèrè.* Why, Señorita, you were of a different opinion yesterday.

*Jasmin.* Yesterday! Yesterday is dead. There's other things to be considered. If you had seen my wedding-presents you'd wonder I talk of Falcon.

*Erèrè.* Have you so many?

*Jasmin.* Erèrè, I am almost crazy trying to count them. And as for knowing what they are for, the Wise Men who gave the first presents would be puzzled. There's everything in the world to wear that sparkles with fire, everything that dances with light, and my heart glows and my feet dance, dance as I try one piece after another on, until I am mad with joy at my bargain. Come now, what can your Falcon give more than this?

*Erèrè.* Nothing!

*Jasmin.* Nothing?

*Erèrè.* No! He'll do better by you than make you presents. He'll allow you to love him to your heart's desire. What girl worth the name would not rather throw her soul, pieced out with her body, at her lover's feet than take an empire from his hands?

*Jasmin.* Oh, that! That's true too. And anyhow, he'll write poems to me.

*Erèrè.* Not after you are married. But he'll read you the verses he writes to other women.

*Jasmin.* Mercy o' me!

*Erèrè.* Jasmin, Jasmin, do not throw this chance away! You may marry Falcon, you may take care of him, and yet you hesitate. Why, child, he has no bed, and your arm shall be his pillow. The world is against him, and your breast shall be his shield. He is poor, and your heart shall be his riches. Here's an opportunity to be the man's whole round of fate,—his providence, his prosperity, his paradise,—and you stand in doubt, stand cold as a midnight fountain.

*Jasmin.* No indeed, Erèrè. I am sure I like Falcon well enough.

*Erèrè.* Think of the hundred ways you may serve him. Think of the thousand ways you may suffer for him. He'll be all your own, and the hungrier and more ragged you grow the more will you inherit in him. You will earn the right to wait on his melancholy or his mirth with silent ministrations. What more could a girl ask?

*Jasmin.* Silence! There's no fun in that. I'd rather tell lies than keep silence.

*Erèrè.* Oh, come with me and let us find Falcon!

*Jasmin.* In a moment. You spoke

of hunger. Do you think I shall be hungry?

*Erèrè.* I am certain of it. And sick too. Nothing shall be wanting to fulfil your fondness. Why do you edge away?

*Jasmin.* And he won't give me one little diamond?

*Erèrè.* Diamonds would spoil all. Where are you going?

*Jasmin.* Wait for me a little, Erèrè. I must go and study out my felicity alone. There ought to be oracles to consult on such occasions. Good-by, Erèrè.

*Erèrè.* Now if my master were only here to seize the golden moment!

*Enter* FALCON.

Why, so he comes. And yawning, rubbing his eyes! Señor, Señor, you have never been asleep on your bridal eve! Is this your ardor, your impatience? Here's Jasmin dying for love of you; one moment burning with blushes, the next bathed in tears. And you sleeping like a slug in the wood! If you waste time thus there'll be no elopement to-night.

*Falcon.* Nor am I sure there will be.

*Erère.* What, not elope! Why, the stars whisper from their mysterious strings an admonition to elope. The moon careers in full cry through heaven, and that's its message. The winds sing, the leaves lisp the word. Every forest path is an invitation, every shady covert a demand that you instantly leave all other business and elope.

*Falcon.* Well, then, I will, but I must change my companion. Will you choose another for me?

*Erère.* What do you say? I will attend you in a moment. Here comes Jasmin back. Stand where you are. Nay, if you run away I'll set Palacios on you.

*Re-enter* JASMIN.

Oh, Jasmin, this is a happy hour! Here is Señor Falcon on his knees to you.

*Jasmin.* I come back to speak to you, Erèrè, but I can go away again. Please let me go away.

*Erèrè.* Not till we have this out. Señor Falcon, your hand. Dear children, I have been a poor carrier-pigeon for your great correspondence. You neither of you know how much you love each other. Now (*joining their hands*) make your own testimony and avouchment.

*Jasmin.* Erèrè, I hear somebody calling me from the house. I must go away. Señor, please let go my hand.

*Falcon.* Señorita, please let go of mine. Erèrè, Pacifico awaits me.

[*Exit* FALCON *and* JASMIN, *separately.*

*Erèrè.* Have both my love-birds flown? Well, I'll be a missionary of marriage no longer. If somebody would only persuade me! Those who are willing are not wanted, and desire follows after denial.

*Enter* PADRE CYPRIAN *and* PADRE PA-
CIFICO.

*Cyprian.* Find me thick shadows. They fit my mood best.

*Pacifico.* Content you, dear brother, content you. Oh, if I could only remember that passage in my Easter sermon in which I describe the brief and blasting glory of mortal passion, 'twould do you good! 'Tis in the style of St. Augustine after he forsook the companionship of girls.

*Cyprian.* What spirit starts before us? 'Tis moonlight made marble,— a ghost with glad eyes. Erèrè!

*Erèrè.* Gentle fathers, I salute you.

*Pacifico.* Dear child, good-night. Now is the flame drawn into the fire. Will you come away, Cyprian?

*Cyprian.* No, let me stay. I will be calm, calm as one about to die. Erèrè, how old are you?

*Erèrè.* Fifteen, Padre Cyprian.

*Cyprian.* So young, so good. Youth is beautiful, but it is not wise; it is not kind, and you are both. Angels are of no age.

*Erèrè.* Alas, Padre, you mistake me. If you or Padre Pacifico would hear me confess, I blush to think what I have to tell.

*Cyprian.* Talk not of confessions to me. Were you born in Ceara?

*Erèrè.* Yes, Padre.

*Cyprian.* I know not why I ask. Near the sea-shore?

*Erèrè.* Yes. Where the waves trailed in and out like the rustling skirts of a great garment.

*Cyprian.* Played you with the sea?

*Erèrè.* Why, as I would with you. I ran among the rocks and peered in

the half-empty caves and dared some
monster to seize me.

*Cyprian.* Monster! Oh, heaven!

*Erèrè.* Are you sick, dear Padre?

*Cyprian.* Yes, child, but with
no known ill. There is a subtle
poison working in me. Perhaps
you have the antidote. You love
Señor Falcon, do you not?

*Erèrè.* Why, I follow him, but why
should I love him? He cheapens
women. If he should cut his finger
he would use a woman instead of a
cobweb to mend it. Oh, I love him
not!

*Cyprian.* He is good to look at.

*Erèrè.* Oh, Padre, the first time I
saw him I thought the sun had come
down into the street! When he went
away it was dark, so I followed him.

*Cyprian.* Then you do love him?

*Erèrè.* How do I know whether I
love him or not. He has not asked
me.

*Cyprian.* Well, you have given me my antidote. Pacifico, come here; I have something to tell you both.

*Pacifico.* Ha! you look more cheerful. You smile. I knew counsel would cure you.

*Cyprian.* Brother, I know your heart. You have loved me and served me. Now you must love me and pray for me. I go on a long journey. Seven hundred miles in the interior of these woods there is a tribe of wild Indians. I have been among them. They know me, and I will save them to the church. To-night I return to our quarters; procure me what things I need, and before daybreak I will be on my way to my distant Mission. Farewell, then, brother; Erèrè, farewell.

*Pacifico.* Why, they are cannibals, Cyprian. You will be eaten, and they are bad cooks too. What insanity is this? You have no flesh to spare to feed Indians with. The moon has got into your brain and you jest with us.

*Cyprian.* It is earnest, Pacifico, but whether sad and serious or merry and pleasant, I know not.

*Pacifico.* What am I to do if you desert me? You know you are the soul of our partnership. Alone, I am only a beast trampling the grass. Suppose they come at me with great questions, how shall I answer them if I have not you to run to? Suppose I fall myself, as may be, who shall pull me up erect? Oh, forgive me, Cyprian, that I deemed you too a sinner! Fire cleanses itself, and your spirit is a never-ceasing flame. But do not leave me. 'Tis Pacifico implores, 'tis your old comrade prays to you.

*Cyprian.* Pacifico, it must be. Say no more. Erèrè, I have one last word for you.

*Erèrè.* Dear Padre, I attend you.

*Cyprian.* You are a woman. You may think more kindly of me when I am gone if you know my secret. I came upon you in the prison, Erèrè, and I saw your soul sitting in your eyes in dumb divineness, and I loved you. Since then the very elements of my nature have been at war to wreck me. My vows and your devotion have preserved my reason. But I must fly from the peril of your face. There must be no dying adieus and echoes of departure, but separation and instant silence.

*Erèrè.* Alas! I can say nothing.

*Pacifico.* Oh, dearest brother, do you go so quickly? I have a hundred riddles for you to unravel before you depart. To think that the brightest ornament of our order must make a mess for cannibals. They will cook you, Cyprian, to a certainty they will cook you. Well, I will go

some way with you.   Alas, alas,
what emptiness must come out of
my mouth hereafter!

[*Exit* PADRE CYPRIAN *and* PADRE
PACIFICO.

*Erèrè.* I am amazed and wonder.

*Re-enter* FALCON.

*Falcon.* Hat in hand and on my
knee, Erèrè, I salute you.

*Erèrè.* Señor, Señor, you mock me!

*Falcon.* Not I!   I am certainly a
fool, and by conjecture a madman,
but I am serious at last.   What you
have seen has been the folly of my
wit.   Marry me, Erèrè, and I will
study stupidity until the world shall
cry " How good a husband!"

*Erèrè.* Why, Señor, you are in
love with Jasmin.

*Falcon.* Jasmin!   There is no Jasmin.

*Erèrè.* Alas, how you men change!
I could repeat twenty invocations of

yours to Jasmin.   Well, I suppose to-morrow it will be a third.   Can't you economize on mistresses and only have one every other day?

*Falcon.* You little wretch, I have a mind to beat you.

*Erèrè.* Do you love me so much as that?   What do you think of my hair, Señor Falcon?

*Falcon.* Your hair!  Oh, your hair is well enough.

*Erèrè.* What do you think of my eyes, Señor Falcon?

*Falcon.* Eyes!  Your eyes are eyes. What else should they be?

*Erèrè.* What do you think of my complexion, Señor Falcon?

*Falcon.* Hang your complexion! What do I care for your complexion? If I wasn't in love with you I could find an epithet for every inch of your body; I could run over like that fountain yonder in comparisons.  Do you think I love you in parcels,—that

I have a measured regard for your nose and a deep adoration for your eyebrows? 'Tis you I love: the indomitable, wild thing of grace and daring that is named Erèrè.

*Erèrè.* Well, Señor Falcon, I must look in my index. Pastor, Ignacio, Angel——

*Falcon.* Mistress Erèrè, no more! You may tread on my neck, but you cannot fix a chain on it. Take me or leave me. For all his sins there is an honest gentleman walks in Falcon's shoes, and he'll bide no woman's scorn.

*Erèrè.* Señor Falcon, perhaps you have erred, and perhaps I have not been perfect, but love is in our hearts, and love is divine enough to mend worse faults than ours. If you want me, I am yours. If you don't want me, I am yours. Oh, friend, do not practise on my fondness! or, if you do, let me not know of it.

*Enter* JASMIN *with a casket.*

*Jasmin*. Señor Falcon, Señor Falcon, if I may take this box of jewels I will go with you to-night, else I'll not stir a step.

*Erèrè*. Alas, lady, you are too late! For lack of better company, Señor Falcon will elope with me.

*Jasmin*. With you! Indeed, with you! Well, you wanted him badly enough. Oh, Señor Falcon, how could you treat me thus! I was just about to be over head in love with you, and you desert me for another. 'Tis infamous and very unkind in you. I will tell Señor Palacios, and he will punish you. Alas, what can I do now? I must go back to the house. I must be true to my diamonds.

*Enter* PALACIOS.

*Palacios*. You here, juggler! Twenty of my people are searching the wood for you.

*Falcon.* What do they or you want with me?

*Palacios.* Wait until my men come up and I will tell you what I think of you. Oh, I will fetch them!

*Jasmin.* Señor Palacios, you are not going to leave me with these dangerous people?

*Palacios.* How came you in the moonlight so close with them? What have you in your hand?

*Jasmin.* Some of my wedding jewels, Señor Palacios. I brought them out to comfort me when you were so piteously stolen from me an hour ago.

*Palacios.* Maybe so! Maybe so!

*Jasmin.* Oh, Señor, you do not suspect me?

*Palacios.* I suspect the world. I suspect humanity. Look at to-night's doings. Out of the nobleness of my heart I entertained this company. I showed them how I live. I hid nothing of my magnificence from them. What is my return? I have been ridiculed, beaten, abused. Henceforth I separate myself from the world. I take my share of fortune's gifts, and mankind may have the rest.

*Jasmin.* Oh, very well, Señor Palacios. I will not sue to you. You will never know what a heart this was till too late.

*Palacios.* Dearest Jasmin, you know I love you.

*Jasmin.* I can go into a convent. Yes, indeed! I can be a nun and wear crawly crape things. There's ways enough! It is more than likely I will die young. You will not be troubled with my fondness, Señor Palacios.

*Palacios.* Sweet, you are unjust. Shall you and I care for nobody in the world but ourselves? Shall we have an heir to make the next generation hate us? So we shall. But you must love me always.

*Jasmin.* Oh, how can I help it, Señor?

*Palacios.* And you must love my things,—this garden—my house—the jewels I have given you.

*Jasmin.* I do! I will!

*Enter* Señora Herrara *and the* Marquis Luna de Silva.

*Señora Herrara.* Jasmin, Jasmin, you unfortunate girl! Wandering in these labyrinths alone and nobody knows what has happened to you.

*Palacios.* Jasmin is safe, madam. I will take care of Jasmin.

*Señora Herrara.* Is that you, son-in-law? I am so used to gazing up at tall people that I overlooked you by a head. Marquis, here is Señor Palacios.

*Palacios.* Madam, I thank you for

your condescension.  Are you all here?  Is Señor Herrara here?

*Señora Herrara.* He comes, and that dear Padre Pacifico with him. Oh, how I adore talent!

*Enter* HERRARA *and* PACIFICO.

*Palacios.* Jasmin, give me leave a moment.  You who are assembled here, one word with all of you.  It is my fault that all these things have happened.  I have forgot myself.  I have been easy and equal with you. You may almost have fancied I was no better than one of yourselves. But that hour is over.  Palacios rules in this house.  Jasmin is mine, but for the rest of you I care not if you take the other three corners of the earth for your habitation.  For you, Señor Poet, I desire you to lift your feet. They don't take root in my garden. This marriage of mine is a prose marriage, a matter-of-fact marriage.

We want a ring, but not a ring of rhymes to make it binding. And we don't care for your green couches of Arcadia, either. Our beds are good enough. To eat well, to have somebody to kiss and somebody else to kick,—there's life for you, and that's an end on 't. So march, and get a market for your moonshine elsewhere. As for you, Marquis Luna de Silva, I beg you to follow him and go farther. Jasmin shall have all the diamonds and dresses she wants, but there shall be no nobility in my house. We shall eat off of gold plate, but, thank God, we'll have no good manners. For you, madam, you can do as you please. Jasmin and I are going into a corner to court, which you have kept us from doing so far. This way, Jasmin; follow me! [*Exit.*

*Jasmin.* Well, mother, you are routed, horse and foot, that's plain.

17

I've got to go with the victor. Adios, Señor Falcon. I will see you again. I will make my husband love you.                    [*Exit.*

*Herrara.* Do you hear, wife? I told you how this would turn out. It's all your fault, Señor Marquis, strutting about with your beggarly airs of importance like somebody from another planet. It is not enough to have common sense in the world and the richest man at the head of the table, but we must bring in the distinctions and the dignities of dreams to confuse all solid order. Where would I be if these things were of any use? I will go after Palacios and appease him. I would not lose his trade for a dozen daughters or a myriad of Marquisates.

                    [*Exit.*

*Señora Herrara.* Never mind, Marquis. The day is not yet lost. Wait till they are married. Jasmin is my daughter, and our race is born to rule. Let us follow Herrara and prevent mischief.

[*Exit* MARQUIS LUNA DE SILVA *and* SEÑORA HERRARA.

*Pacifico.* Well, my children, the generation of the world dismisses us. We are driven from the pleasant places of the earth to find a refuge in the desert. 'Tis they are the poorer for losing us. Let us go. I'll not part with you till I see you married. Come, Falcon; come, Erèrè. I'll love you for Cyprian's sake. You twin stars, what have you to complain of who have just come into the inheritance of each other? But I,—my soul is torn from me and hurried into the thick woods. I am a lifeless trunk that rots to dust.

*Erèrè.* Dear Padre, we will make you bud and bloom again. Give him your hand, Falcon.

*Falcon.* Cheer up, Padre. Come,

Erèrè. I will take you home to Cerita. I will get you the palace washing to do, and all will yet be well.

THE END.

www.ingramcontent.com/pod-product-compliance
Lightning Source LLC
Chambersburg PA
CBHW030550040726
47497CB00008B/2650